Enid Blyton®

THE FAMOUS FIVE

ADVENTURE GAME BOOK 6

An Enid Blyton story devised and adapted by Mary Danby

Illustrated by Gavin Rowe

A division of Hachette Children's Books

First published in Great Britain in 1988 by Hodder and Stoughton

This revised edition first published in 2011 by Hodder Children's Books

1

A Catalogue record for this book is available from the British Library

ISBN 978 1 444 90324 9

Typeset in Legacy Serif by Avon DataSet Ltd, Bidford-on-Avon, Warwickshire

Printed and bound in Great Britain by Clays Ltd, St Ives plc

The paper and board used in this paperback by Hodder Children's Books
are natural recyclable products made from wood grown in sustainable
forests. The manufacturing processes conform to the environmental
regulations of the country of origin.

Hodder Children's Books
a division of Hachette Children's Books
338 Euston Road, London NW1 3BH
An Hachette UK company
www.hachette.co.uk

THE FAMOUS FIVE

Adventure Game Book

Unlike an ordinary book, which you can read straight through from beginning to end, this is a game book, in which *you* choose how the story should go.

Begin at section number **1**. At the end of each section you are told which section to read next. Sometimes you will find you have a choice. (For instance, at the end of section 9 you have to decide whether or not George should try to hide Timmy from her headmistress.)

Every time you have a choice to make, there will be one way that is the quickest and best – and you have to guess (or work out, if you can) which it is. If you choose the wrong section, you can still carry on reading, but when you find yourself back at the main story you will find you have picked up a few 'red herrings'.

A red herring is the name given to something

that carries you away from the main subject (as when someone is telling you a story and puts in all sorts of details that don't really matter). Your aim is to try and stay on the main track, without going off down the little side roads.

See if you can make the right choices and find your way to the end of the story without picking up too many red herrings. Red herrings are represented in the text by a symbol: 🐟. (Use a pencil and paper to add up your score as you go along.) Then turn to the back of the book to see how well the Famous Five (and you) have done.

1

Anne was trying to do some history revision in a corner of the school common room when her cousin George came bursting in.

George was not a boy. She was a girl called Georgina, but because she had always wanted to be a boy she insisted on being called George. She wore her curly hair cut short, and her bright blue eyes gleamed angrily.

'Anne! I've just had a letter from home - and guess what? Dad wants to go and live on my island to do some special work - and he wants to build a sort of tower on it!'

The other girls looked up in amusement, and Anne held out her hand for the letter that George was waving at her. Everyone knew about the little island off Kirrin Bay that belonged to George.

Kirrin Island was a tiny place with an old ruined castle in the middle of it, the home of rabbits and gulls and jackdaws.

It had underground dungeons in which George and her cousins had had some amazing adventures. It had once belonged to George's mother, who had given it to George - and George was very fierce where her precious island was concerned! It was *hers*. Nobody else could live there, or even land on it without permission.

And now, here was her father proposing to build some sort of workshop on her island. George was red with exasperation.

Go to **5**.

2

'I bet they *have* gone to have something to eat! You know what Dick's like – always hungry,' said George.

'Yes, but Julian said they would meet us right here,' said Anne. 'Do you think they've missed their train?'

'Nobody can miss a school train,' said George witheringly. 'The masters would check that all the boys were on the coach before it left school! Come on, let's go and have something to eat anyway. If the boys aren't in the snack bar, I'll eat my hat!'

Anne glanced at George's black felt school hat and grinned. She had a vision of George munching the brim, and it made her giggle all the way to the snack bar door.

Leaving Timmy outside, the girls went in.

'Oh, look,' said George, as she closed the door. 'There they are!'

Go to **6**.

3

The headmistress had nearly reached them, and George knew that she would have to try and bluff her way out of the situation. She stood still, waiting for the headmistress to speak to her. Miss Abbott stopped, and frowned at George.

'Why are you trying to bring your dog into the school?' she demanded. 'You know that pets are not allowed in the main school buildings!'

'Well, I went out to check that he had plenty of water, and he followed me back into the building,' explained George.

It was perfectly true, she thought. Timmy *had* followed her back to the school.

'Take him back to the pets' yard,' ordered the headmistress. 'Quickly, now!'

'Yes, Miss Abbott,' said George meekly.

The headmistress didn't move. She was obviously waiting for George to take Timmy back to his kennel.

Go to **7**.

4

George cheered up at Julian's sensible words. There *were* a great many things they could do apart from going over to her island. They could go for long walks over the moors behind the house, visit old friends like Mr and Mrs Sanders, who lived on a nearby farm, and even go into the town occasionally.

'I hope Mum brought the pony trap to the station,' said George, as the train started to slow down for Kirrin. 'It's much more fun than the car.'

'I think she'll have to come in the car,' said Julian. 'The five of us *and* our luggage *and* Aunt Fanny might be a bit much for the pony!'

'There she is!' shouted Anne, leaning out of the window. 'Hello, Aunt Fanny! How are you? How's Uncle Quentin?'

'Very well, last time I saw him,' said her aunt,

kissing first George and then Anne.

'I can't wait to see the tower he's built on my island,' said George. 'Come on, Mum, let's hurry home.'

'I'd like to go into the town and have an ice-cream,' said Dick, 'to celebrate the start of the holidays! May we do that, Aunt Fanny?'

If you think they should go straight to Kirrin Cottage, go to **11**.
If you think they should go into the town, go to **17**.

5

Anne read the letter. It was from George's mother:

'My dear George,

I think I must tell you at once that your father proposes to live on Kirrin Island for some time in order to finish some very important experiments he is making. He will have to have some kind of building erected there – a sort of tower, I believe. Apparently he needs a place

where he can have absolute peace and isolation, and also, for some reason, where there is water all around him. The fact of being surrounded by water is necessary to his experiments.

Don't be upset about this, please. I know that you consider Kirrin Island is your very own, but you must allow your family to share it, especially when it is for something as important as your father's scientific work. Dad thinks you will be very pleased indeed to lend him Kirrin Island, but I know you have strong feeling about it, so I thought I had better write and tell you, before you arrive home and see him installed there.'

Anne looked at George.

'Oh, George! I don't see why you mind your father borrowing Kirrin Island for a bit! I wouldn't mind *my* father doing something like that!'

'*Your* father would ask you first,' said George sulkily. 'My father just does exactly as he likes without asking if anyone minds. I really do think he might have written to me himself.'

She took back the letter and read it again gloomily.

'To think that all my lovely holiday plans are spoilt!' she said. 'You know how brilliant Kirrin Island is at Easter – the primroses will be out, and there will be lots of baby rabbits. You and Julian and Dick are coming to stay, too, and we haven't had a holiday together since we went caravanning last summer.'

Go to **9**.

6

Two boys in school uniform were at the counter, buying buns and lemonade.

'Julian! Dick!' called Anne, but the boys didn't turn round.

Anne blushed. They had made a silly mistake. It wasn't her brothers after all.

'They did look *quite* like Julian and Dick – from the back, anyway,' said George. 'Oh well, here goes!' She pretended to chew her hat, much to the surprise of two old ladies drinking tea near by.

'Come on,' said Anne. 'Let's get back. The boys are probably looking for us.'

They made their way back to the platform.

Go to **16**.

7

George opened the back door and ushered Timmy outside.

'Come on, Timmy!' she said, and set off along the path to the pets' yard. The headmistress watched her from the open door for a moment, then swept off to supper.

George still felt miserable about her father using Kirrin Island. She was longing to have Timmy's comforting body on her feet that night. What a nuisance she had run into Miss Abbott!

Suddenly she turned round and headed back towards the main school. She *must* have Timmy with her – she simply must.

'We'll try again, Tim,' she said to the big dog, 'but if I get caught this time, there'll be real trouble!'

She opened the back door and glanced quickly up and down the corridor. It was empty.

'Come on, Timmy,' she hissed. 'Quickly!'

Go to **15**.

8

Julian saw their trunks into the guard's van, then joined the others on the train.

'I hope you're not going to go up in smoke over this business of your father using Kirrin Island for his experiments,' Julian said to George as the train pulled out. 'You've got to realise that your father is a brilliant man – someone whose work is of real benefit to people, and I think you should be proud of that, and be happy to help him by letting him use your island if he wants to.'

George scratched Timmy's head and looked thoughtful.

'All right,' she said at last. 'I'll try not to make a fuss about it – but I'm so disappointed.'

'We're all disappointed,' replied her cousin, 'but we'll have to put up with it. After all, there are lots of other things we can do during the holidays.'

Go to **4**.

9

'Perhaps your father wouldn't mind if we went and stayed on Kirrin Island anyway?' suggested Anne. 'We wouldn't disturb him.'

'It wouldn't be anything like as good as being there on our own,' retorted George scornfully. 'You know how irritable Dad can be when he's busy.'

Well, yes – Anne did know. George's father was a famous and brilliant scientist, but he was also a hot-tempered and impatient man. When he was in the middle of one of his experiments he was unbearable. The least noise upset him.

'Well, don't spend the rest of the day brooding about it,' said Anne. 'Go down to the kennels and see Timmy. He'll soon cheer you up.'

Timmy was George's dog, a big black and white mongrel whom she loved with all her heart. Graylands School allowed the girls to keep their pets at school, otherwise George would never have agreed to go there. She couldn't bear to be parted from Timmy, even for a day.

She went out to the big yard where Timmy had his kennel, and sat talking to him and stroking him for a long time. On impulse, she decided to take him into the school building and up to the dormitory, so that he could sleep on her bed that night, as he always did when they were at home. The girls were forbidden to have pets in the main school building, but that didn't worry George!

She took Timmy to the back door of the school. Peering round it, she saw that the long corridor that led to the cloakrooms was empty.

'Come on, Timmy!' she called, and the big dog followed her into the corridor. Just then, to George's horror, she saw Miss Abbott, the headmistress, coming down the corridor towards her!

In a panic, George tried to decide what to do. Should she try and bluff her way out of trouble, or should she push Timmy back outside the door, and hope Miss Abbott hadn't seen him?

If you think she should bluff, go to paragraph **3**.

If you think she should push Timmy outside, go to paragraph **12**.

10

At last the end of term came. George, Anne and Timmy were taken to the station by the school coach. They were to travel to London, where they would meet Julian and Dick, whose train arrived just before theirs.

Anne leant so far out of the windows as the train pulled into the station that George grabbed hold of her skirt and hauled her back.

'Careful!' she said. 'You don't want to injure yourself at the start of the holidays, do you?'

'I'm trying to spot the boys,' said Anne. 'Their train has obviously arrived, because there are masses of boys in uniform on the platform, but I can't pick out Julian and Dick.'

The two girls got out of the train, followed by Timmy, who gambolled round and round them as they struggled up the platform, carrying their luggage. They looked round for Julian and Dick, but there was no sign of them.

'I'll bet they've gone to have something to eat,' said George. 'I think we should go and look for them in the station snack bar.'

'Well, Julian said in his last letter that they would wait for us on the platform, so I think we should stay here,' objected Anne.

If you think they should go to the snack bar, go to **2**.
If you think they should wait on the platform, go to **16**.

11

Aunt Fanny smiled with pleasure at seeing them all again. 'Hello, boys! How are you? Did you have a good term? We must go straight home, Dick. I've got a lot to do. We'll go into the town for an ice-cream some other time. Come on, I've brought the trap.'

She led the way through the booking hall to where the pony trap was waiting.

'I thought you would have come in the car, Aunt Fanny,' said Julian. 'What about our trunks - they won't fit in here!'

'Mr Sanders said he would bring them up later on,' replied his aunt. 'It's such a beautiful day I thought you'd enjoy a ride in the trap.'

'How's Dad?' asked George.

'He's very well,' said her mother. 'I've never known him to be so thrilled as he has been lately. His work has been coming along very well.'

'I suppose you don't know what he's doing?' asked Dick.

'Oh, no,' Aunt Fanny answered. 'He never says a word about it to me, but I understand that it's very important. Of course, I do know the last part of the experiment has to be carried out in a place that is surrounded by deep water.'

Go to **24**.

12

George wrenched the door open again and shoved Timmy outside. Slamming the door, she stood still, politely waiting for the headmistress to pass.

'Have you been out to see Timmy?' asked Miss Abbott, pausing in front of George, who felt herself going red.

'Y-yes, Miss Abbott,' she replied. 'I – er – wanted to check he had some fresh water.'

'You take very good care of that dog, George,' said the headmistress. 'I'm pleased to see that you are so responsible.'

'Thank you, Miss Abbott,' replied George, trying not to smile.

The headmistress nodded and swept away down the corridor. George waited until she was out of sight, then opened the door again.

'Come on, Timmy,' she hissed. 'Quickly!'

Go to **15**.

13

The four children and Timmy tore in at the front gate, and clattered through the house and up to their rooms. Anne sighed with pleasure at seeing her old room again, with its two windows, one looking on to the moor at the back of the house, and the other sideways on to the sea. She had started to unpack her bag when she heard Aunt Fanny calling.

'Children! Tea's ready!'

Aunt Fanny had prepared an enormous tea, knowing how hungry they always were after the journey from school, but there was very little left on the table by the time the four of them had finished!

'Oh, it's brilliant to be back,' said Anne later that evening, as she got into bed.

Timmy, who was already lying curled up on George's feet, thumped his tail as if in agreement!

Go to **21**.

14

It didn't take very long to reach the town, and Aunt Fanny managed to find a parking space in the main street.

'I'll only be about ten minutes,' she said as she got out of the car.

Dick could see a shop that sold ice-cream on the opposite side of the road.

'Have you got any money, Ju?' he asked.

'A bit,' said Julian. 'Why?'

'I thought we could have an ice-cream – there's a shop that sells them over there.'

Julian felt in his pocket and pulled out a few coins.

'Here you are,' he said.

Dick took the coins and opened the car door. Timmy was still sitting across his lap, and Dick gave him a push to make him move. Unfortunately he pushed too hard, and Timmy fell out on to the pavement!

'Timmy!' shrieked George, scrambling out of the car. 'Oh, Dick, look what you've done!'

Go to **20**.

15

If you have arrived from paragraph 7, *score* ᗧ.

George hurried Timmy up to her dormitory without further trouble. He scuttled under her bed quickly and lay down.

'Now, lie quiet,' said George, and went to join the other girls. She found Anne busily writing a letter to her brothers, Julian and Dick, who were also at boarding school.

'I've told them about your father using the island, George,' she said. 'You know, there's one good thing about it, we won't have to creep about on tiptoe and whisper, if your father isn't at Kirrin

Cottage. We can be as noisy as we like. Do cheer up, George!'

It took George a long time to get over the fit of gloom caused by her mother's letter. Even having Timmy on her bed every night, until he was discovered by an angry teacher, did not quite make up for her disappointment.

Go to **10**.

16

If you've arrived from **6**, *score* 🐟🐟.

'I suppose we'd better hang around here for a while,' said George reluctantly. 'It's practically impossible to pick anyone out of this crowd!'

Suddenly two boys separated themselves from the crowd on the platform and ran towards the girls.

'Here they are!' said Anne. 'Hi, Julian! Hi, Dick! It's fantastic to see you!'

'Hello, you two!' said Julian. 'Hello, Timmy – have you behaved yourself this term?'

'Well,' said George, 'he only got the roast beef out of the larder once, and he didn't do so much harm to that cushion he chewed – and if people *will* leave their wellies lying around nobody can blame Timmy for chewing them!'

The boys laughed as they all made their way across the station concourse to where the train for Kirrin was waiting.

Go to **8**.

17

'I don't see why not,' said Aunt Fanny, smiling at them all. 'I've brought the car, because the five of you and all your luggage would have been too much for the trap. I've got some shopping to do, anyway, so it would suit me quite well to go into the town now.'

'Shall we load our cases into the car?' asked Julian.

'Yes please, dear,' said his aunt. 'That would be very helpful.'

The children dealt quickly with the cases, then jumped in. Julian sat in the front beside Aunt Fanny, and Timmy lay across the laps of the three children in the back, wagging his tail in George's face!

'Can we have tea as well as an ice-cream in the town, please, Aunt Fanny?' asked Dick.

His aunt smiled. 'No, Dick, I'm afraid not,' she said. 'I've got an enormous tea waiting for you at home.'

Go to **14**.

18

'George, you shouldn't talk to your mother like that,' said Julian.

George took no notice.

'I'm going to tell Dad exactly what I think of him – helping himself to my island!' she shouted.

Aunt Fanny was normally very patient with her difficult daughter, but this time George had gone too far.

'You will apologise for your rudeness, Georgina,' she said firmly.

George remained silent, glowering furiously.

'Very well, you will go to your room and stay there until you do apologise,' said Aunt Fanny firmly. 'You will not come to the island unless you apologise first.'

George rushed out of the room, banging the door behind her. A moment later they heard the door of her bedroom slam. Julian looked at his aunt.

'I'll go and see if I can get her to come and say she's sorry, Aunt Fanny,' he said. 'Why don't you all get ready to go to the island?'

'Oh, thank you, Julian, dear,' said his aunt gratefully.

Julian ran upstairs and tapped on George's door.

'George! Open the door! I want to speak to you!'

Inside the room, George hesitated. She badly wanted to go over to the island, but she didn't want to see anyone. She was so cross!

If you think George should open the door, go to **23**.
If you think she shouldn't, go to **29**.

19

'I'd love to go and see it,' said Anne. 'It looks so strange. Is Uncle Quentin all alone on Kirrin Island, Aunt Fanny?'

'Yes, and I don't like it very much,' said Aunt Fanny. 'For one thing, I'm sure that he doesn't have proper meals, and for another, he would have no way of letting us know if he had an accident.'

'Well, could you arrange for him to signal to you every night and every morning?' suggested Julian. 'He could use that tower, and flash a signal to you in the morning – using a mirror, you know, and at night he could signal with a lamp.'

'Well, I did suggest something of the sort,' replied his aunt, 'but he didn't take any notice. If we go and see him tomorrow, perhaps you could mention it, Julian.'

'Do you mean that Dad really won't mind if we go over and disturb him?' said George in astonishment. 'I thought we'd all have to keep well away.'

'No, he particularly asked me to take you all to the island,' said Aunt Fanny. 'I have to take food and other things that he asks me to get him occasionally. Well, here we are, back at Kirrin Cottage.'

Go to **13**.

20

Timmy struggled to his feet and gave himself a shake. George knelt down beside him, running her hands over his furry body to see if he was hurt.

'Honestly, Dick!' she snapped, glaring at her cousin. 'You really should be more careful. Poor Timmy could have hurt himself quite badly.'

'I'm sorry, George,' said Dick. 'It was an accident. He's all right, though, isn't he?'

'No thanks to you!' said George crossly.

Julian got out of the car.

'You go and get us all some ice-cream, Dick,' he said. 'George, you get into the front with Timmy. Hurry up, Dick, I can see Aunt Fanny coming.'

Dick crossed the road to the shop, and got back to the car just as Aunt Fanny was putting her shopping in the boot.

'Can you manage, Aunt Fanny?' asked Dick. 'There's not much room in the boot with all our trunks in there.'

'I can just squeeze the shopping into this corner,'

replied his aunt. 'Get in, Dick. We'll soon be back at Kirrin Cottage.'

'How's Dad?' asked George, as they left the town.

'He's very well,' said her mother. 'I've never known him to be so thrilled as he has been lately. His work has been coming along very well.'

'I suppose you don't know what he's doing?' asked Dick.

'Oh, no,' Aunt Fanny answered. 'He never says a word about it to me, but I understand that it's very important. Of course, I do know the last part of the experiment has to be carried out in a place that is surrounded by deep water.'

Go to **24**.

21

Next day was fine and warm. 'We can go across to the island this morning,' said Aunt Fanny. 'We'll take our own food, because I'm sure Uncle Quentin will have forgotten we're coming.'

'Does he have a boat there?' asked George. 'Mum, he hasn't taken *my* boat, has he?'

'No, dear,' replied her mother. 'He's got another boat. I was afraid he would never be able to get it in and out of all those dangerous rocks round the island, but he got one of the fishermen to take him, and had his own boat towed behind, with all his stuff in it. Now, George, you must promise me that you won't get angry with your father, no matter what he does or says. You know how irritable he can get while he's working on an important experiment.'

George had promised herself that she wouldn't lose her temper again about her father using the island, but suddenly she saw red.

'I will get angry if I don't like what he's doing!'

she shouted at her mother. 'Dad's got absolutely no right to use the island without asking my permission. You should have stopped him, Mum!'

Go to **18**.

22

'No, it won't!' shouted Julian. 'You can't see – you're facing the wrong way. You're much too close to the rocks!'

George gave a quick glance over her shoulder.

'Oh, no!' she exclaimed, and hauled frantically at the oars, but it was too late! There was a nasty scraping noise as the boat grounded on the rocks.

'Oh, no!' groaned George. 'What a silly thing for me to do!'

Nobody dared say that they agreed with her, in case she lost her temper again, but it was what they were all thinking!

'What are we going to do, George?' asked Julian. 'What's the best way to get the boat off here?'

'Well,' said George, considering the problem, 'provided I haven't holed the bottom of the boat, we might be able to push it off. The only thing is, someone will have to get out of the boat and stand on the rocks to push!'

'OK,' said Julian cheerfully, rolling up the legs of his jeans. 'I've got trainers on – it won't matter if they get wet, and they'll protect my feet.'

'Be careful, Julian . . .' said Aunt Fanny.

Julian swung himself nimbly over the side of the boat, and balanced on the rocks just below the surface. The water was so cold that it made him gasp.

Go to **25**.

23

There was silence for a moment or two, then Julian heard the key turn in the lock. The door opened a crack, and George's flushed face peered round it.

'What do you want?' she snapped.

'Look, why don't you come down and say you're sorry?' said Julian. 'You'll miss going to the island, and we don't want to go without you. Come on, George, *please*.'

George knew she had been rude to her mother, and she desperately wanted to go to Kirrin Island.

'All right,' she said finally.

'Well done,' said Julian. 'I knew you would.'

Julian and George went downstairs. Aunt Fanny was in the kitchen, packing some food to take with them.

'I'm sorry I was rude to you, Mum,' said George in a low voice.

'That's all right,' said her mother, smiling. 'Now, if everyone's ready, we'll go, shall we?'

It only took a few minutes for them to reach the

place where George's boat was moored. They all climbed in, and were soon moving smoothly over the calm water.

Go to **27**.

24

If you've arrived from **20**, *score* 🐟🐟.

'Look! There's Kirrin Island!' said Anne suddenly.

They had rounded a corner and come in sight of the bay. Guarding the entrance to it was the curious little island topped by the old ruined castle. The sun shone down on the blue sea, and the island looked most enchanting.

George gazed earnestly at it. She was looking for the building, whatever it was, that her father said he needed for his work. Everyone looked at the island, seeking the same thing.

They saw it easily enough! Rising from the centre

of the castle, probably from the castle yard, was a tall thin tower, rather like a lighthouse. At the top was a glass enclosed room, which glittered in the sun.

'I don't like it, Mum! It spoils Kirrin Island!' said George in dismay.

'It can come down when your father has finished his work,' said her mother. 'It's a very flimsy, temporary thing. He promised me he would scrap it as soon as his work was done. You can go across and see it if you like. It's really quite interesting.'

Go to **19**.

25

‘Right!’ shouted George. ‘Push!’

Julian pushed as hard as he could, and slowly the boat began to move. Once again there was a nasty scraping as it came off the rocks.

Julian jumped in quickly, and George began to row.

‘How will we know if there’s a hole in the bottom?’ asked Anne, looking worried.

‘The boat will start to leak, and then it’ll sink,’ said Dick brightly.

‘Don’t take any notice of him, Anne,’ said George. ‘We would have known straight away if the boat was letting in water. It’s all right, I promise you.’

Anne looked relieved. The boat moved smoothly on towards the island.

Go to **30**.

26

'Isn't it strange?' said Dick. 'Look at that little glass room at the top. I wonder what it's for? Can anyone climb up inside the tower?' he asked, turning to Aunt Fanny.

'Yes,' replied his aunt. 'There's a narrow staircase inside. That's about all there is inside the tower itself. It's the little room at the top that's important. It's got some extraordinary wiring there, essential to your uncle's experiments. I don't think he does anything with the tower – it just has to *be* there, doing something on its own, which has a certain effect on the experiments he's making.'

The boat ran into the little harbour and grounded softly. There was another boat there already – Uncle Quentin's. George and Julian leapt out and pulled the boat a bit further up the beach, so that Aunt Fanny could get out without wetting her feet. Timmy ran up the beach in delight.

'Now, Timmy,' said George warningly, and Timmy

turned a despairing eye on his mistress. Surely she wasn't going to stop him looking to see if there were any rabbits?

Ah – there was a rabbit! And another, and another!

'They're just as tame as ever!' exclaimed Anne in delight.

Timmy suddenly bounded forward.

'Timmy! Come here at once!' George commanded.

If you think Timmy obeys her, go to **38**.
If you think he doesn't, go to **32**.

27

If you've arrived from **33**, *score* [fish symbol].

'George,' said her mother nervously, as they came near to Kirrin Island, 'you will be careful of these awful rocks, won't you? The water's so clear today that I can see them all – and some of them are only just below the water.'

'Mum, you know I've rowed to Kirrin Island hundreds of times!' laughed George. 'I *couldn't* go on a rock! I know them all, really I do!'

She rowed on strongly, enjoying the sunshine and the salty air. Unfortunately, she was so busy enjoying the beautiful day that she didn't concentrate hard enough on her rowing, and the boat started to veer towards the rocks!

'George! Watch out!' shouted Dick and Julian together. 'You're heading for the rocks! Pull to the left!'

'It's all right,' said George. 'The current will carry us straight past the rocks.'

If you think Dick and Julian are right, go to **22**.
If you think George is right, go to **35**.

28

They passed through an old ruined doorway into a great yard. Once there had been a stone-paved floor, but now most of it was covered by sand, and by close-growing weeds or grass.

The castle had two towers, one of which was almost a complete ruin. The other was in better shape. Jackdaws circled it, and flew above the children's heads, crying 'chack, chack, chack'.

'I suppose Dad must be living in the little room with the two slit-like windows,' said George. 'There isn't anything else – unless he's down in the dungeons!'

'Let's call him,' suggested Dick. They all shouted loudly.

'Uncle Quentin! Where are you?'

No Uncle Quentin appeared. They shouted again.

'UNCLE QUENTIN! WHERE ARE YOU?'

There was no answer.

'Where can he be?' asked Anne in bewilderment.

'I think we'd better have a look round the island,' said Julian.

Go to **31**.

29

There was silence from inside the room.

'George!' called Julian again. 'Open the door.'

'No!' shouted George. 'Now just go away and leave me alone. I don't want to come to Kirrin Island anyway. It's probably completely spoilt with all Dad's stuff on it!'

Julian shrugged his shoulders and went downstairs again. There were times when George wouldn't listen to anyone!

The three children and Aunt Fanny got ready to leave the house. Aunt Fanny called up to George to tell her they were going, but got no reply.

It was a beautiful day – warm and sunny, without a cloud in the sky, and the sea was flat calm. They walked along the beach to where George's boat was moored. Just as they got up to it, Aunt Fanny suddenly gasped.

'What is it, Aunt Fanny?' asked Anne. 'Have you forgotten something?'

'No, it's not that,' replied her aunt. 'I've just realised that George is the only one who knows the way round to the little mooring place on Kirrin Island!'

Go to **33**.

30

If you've arrived from **25**, *score* 🐟.

There was only one place to land safely on the island. This was a little cove, a natural harbour running up to a stretch of sand. It was sheltered by high rocks all round. George worked her way to the east side of the island, rounded a low wall of very sharp rocks, and there lay the cove, a smooth inlet of water running into the shore.

Anne had been looking at the island as George rowed. There was the old ruined castle in the centre, with its tumbledown towers full of jackdaws as usual. The walls were covered with ivy.

'It's a lovely place,' said Anne with a sigh. Then she gazed at the curious tower that now rose from the centre of the castle yard. It was not built of brick, but of some smooth, shiny material that was fitted together in sections. Evidently the tower had been made in that way so that it might be brought to the island easily, and set up there quickly.

Go to **26**.

31

Leaving Aunt Fanny sitting in the sunshine in the courtyard, the children went to look in the little room first. Much to their surprise, not only was

Uncle Quentin not there, there was nothing at all in the room!

'That's strange,' said George. 'Do you think he's down in the dungeons after all? Come on, let's go and see.'

As they went towards the dungeons, they expected to see the big stone that covered the entrance standing upright, so that they could go down the steps underground, but it was lying flat. Julian was just about to pull on the iron ring to lift it up when he noticed something strange.

Go to **36**.

32

If you've arrived from **38**, *score* 🐟.

Timmy, unable to resist the temptation, raced towards the surprised rabbits. In an instant nothing could be seen but white tails flashing up and down as rabbit after rabbit rushed to its burrow.

'Oh, Timmy!' called George crossly.

'Where's Uncle Quentin?' asked Anne, as they walked to the great broken archway that was the entrance to the old castle. Behind it were the stone steps that led towards the centre. They were cracked and irregular now. Aunt Fanny went across them carefully, but the children, who were wearing rubber-soled shoes, ran over them quickly.

Go to **28**.

33

Back at Kirrin Cottage, George was gazing out of her bedroom window, wishing she could go to Kirrin Island too. She had tried very hard not to make a fuss about the way her father had taken over the island, but it had got too much for her, and so she had shouted at her mother.

'I do wish I could go over to the island,' she said

to herself. 'It will be brilliant on the sea today – it's so warm and sunny.'

Suddenly George sat up straight, with a very mischievous look on her face.

'They won't be able to go over to the island without me! I'm the only one who can negotiate the rocks and get safely to the little creek where we moor the boat!' she thought.

George scrambled off the bed.

'Come on, Timmy!' she said. 'We'd better go and find the others, or Mum might let Julian row out to the island, and he could easily damage my boat on the rocks. He doesn't know the way, even though he can row very well.'

It only took a few minutes for George and Timmy to catch up with the others on the beach.

'George! I thought I told you to stay in your room,' said her mother. 'But I'm glad you've come, because we need you to navigate the boat safely round the rocks.'

'I know,' grinned George. 'That's why I came down after you. I'm very sorry I was rude to you, Mum.'

'That's all right, dear,' said her mother. 'Now, in you all get.'

They piled into the boat, and were soon moving smoothly over the water.

Go to **27**.

34

'Better not touch them,' said Julian, 'they might be live. I think I'd better go up the top on my own first, to see what's up there. If it's safe, I'll call you.'

He began to climb the steep, spiral stairway. It made him quite giddy to go round and round, up and up, so many times. The others followed him. Tiny, slit-like windows were let into the side of the tower here and there, and gave a little light to the stairway. Julian looked through one, and had a wonderful view of the sea and the mainland.

He went on to the top. When he got there he found himself in a small round room, whose sides were of thick, gleaming glass. Wires ran right into the glass itself, and then pierced through it, the free ends waving and glittering in the strong wind that blew round the tower.

There was nobody in the little room, though. Uncle Quentin clearly was only using it to carry the wires up to the top so that they could wave in the air. Julian wondered, frowning, what was the meaning of the tower and the thin, shining wires?

Go to **41**.

35

The two boys watched as George stopped rowing. Just as they thought the boat was sure to hit the rocks, it slipped sideways past them. George lowered the oars into the water again, and once more the boat skimmed swiftly towards Kirrin Island.

'I thought you said you couldn't possibly go on the rocks!' teased Dick, with a grin.

‘I *didn’t*!’ said George crossly.

‘Yes, but it was a near thing, wasn’t it?’ said Dick.

George scowled at him, but then had to smile. It was too nice a day to be cross with anyone.

Go to **30**.

36

‘Look,’ he said. ‘There are weeds growing round the edges of the stone. Nobody has lifted it for a long time. Uncle Quentin can’t be in the dungeons!’

The four children stared at each other in bewilderment.

‘Well,’ said Dick at last, ‘the only other place where he might be is the big cave we hid in once, but he would have to drop into that through the hole in the roof – or scramble over the rocks. He’d never have been able to get all his equipment into it. I don’t think he can be there.’

‘I don’t know,’ said Julian doubtfully. ‘He *might*

be. Perhaps we should go and have a look to make sure.'

'I think we should look inside the funny tower,' argued Dick.

If you think they should look in the cave, go to **49**.

If you think they should go to the tower, go to **43**.

37

George was right behind her, and grabbed her arm before she could fall.

'Sorry, Anne,' she said. 'That was very naughty of Timmy. Are you all right?'

'Yes, thanks,' said Anne, holding the rail tightly as she made her way down the remaining steps.

They all went over to where Aunt Fanny was sitting.

Go to **42**.

38

Timmy put his tail down and looked round at George miserably.

'Good boy. Come here,' she said, reaching to pat him.

'Look!' said Aunt Fanny, pointing out to sea. 'I wonder where that boat's going?'

A white speedboat was just passing the island, throwing up twin plumes of spray behind it. Standing at the wheel was a man with a red beard. When he saw he was being watched, he turned the wheel and swept out to sea.

While they were all busy gazing at the retreating boat, another little family of rabbits came hopping into the cove.

Go to **32**.

39

Julian was soon in the cave. A dim light came in from the seaward side. He took a quick look round. There was absolutely nothing there at all, except for an old box they must have left behind when they were last here themselves.

He climbed up the rope again. Dick gave him a hand.

'Well?' he said. 'Any sign of Uncle Quentin?'

'No,' said Julian. 'He's not there, and hasn't been, either. It's a mystery! Where is he, and if he's doing really important work, where is his equipment? After all, we know that plenty of stuff was brought here, because Aunt Fanny told us so!'

'I think we'd better go and check the funny tower,' said Dick.

Go to **43**.

Everyone stared at Uncle Quentin. He was watching the jackdaws intently, and hadn't noticed his wife or the children.

Timmy leapt to his feet, and gambolled over to George's father. He barked loudly. Uncle Quentin jumped, and turned round. He saw Timmy – and then he saw all the others, staring at him in astonishment.

Uncle Quentin didn't look particularly pleased to see anyone. He walked slowly towards them,

a slight frown on his face.

'This is a surprise,' he said. 'I had no idea that you were all coming today.'

'Oh, *Quentin*!' said his wife reproachfully. 'I wrote it down for you in your diary. You know I did.'

'Did you? Well, I haven't looked at my diary since, so it's no wonder I forgot,' said Uncle Quentin, a little peevishly. He kissed his wife, George and Anne, and shook hands with the boys.

'Uncle Quentin, where did you come from?' asked Dick, who was eaten up with curiosity.

Go to **44**.

41

What a marvellous view there was from the windows! He could see miles and miles out to sea – and on the other side of the tower, miles and miles across the bay, over the mainland to the hills beyond.

'Hey, Julian!' shouted Dick. 'What on earth are you doing up there? Can we come up?'

'Yes,' Julian called back, 'but George had better leave Timmy down there. I don't think there'll be room for him up here as well.'

'Oh, nonsense!' shouted George. 'You know he won't want to stay down here without me, Ju!'

If you think George should take Timmy up the tower, go to **47**.
If you think she should leave him on the ground, go to **53**.

42

If you've arrived from **37**, *score* 🐟.

'Well, did you see anything interesting up there?' asked Aunt Fanny.

'There was a marvellous view from the top,' answered Anne, 'but no sign of Uncle Quentin. It's very mysterious, Aunt Fanny – we really have looked everywhere we thought he could be – but he's just not here.'

'It does seem strange,' agreed Aunt Fanny, 'but you don't know your uncle as well as I do. He always turns up all right. He's probably forgotten that we were coming.'

'Well, it's very odd,' began Dick, and then stopped suddenly. A curious noise came to their ears – a rumbling, grumbling, angry noise, like a giant dog growling in fury. There was a hissing noise from the tower, and all the wires that stuck out at the top were suddenly lit up as if by lightning!

Go to **46**.

43

If you've arrived from **39**, *score* 🐟 🐟.

'Perhaps you're right, Dick,' said Julian. 'Come on, let's go to the tower. I hope it isn't locked!'

Fortunately the key was in the lock. Julian turned it and unlocked the door, which opened outwards, not inwards. He put his head inside and looked around.

There was not much room inside. A spiral staircase, made of the same shiny stuff as the tower itself, wound up and up. There was a space at one side of it, into which projected curious hook-like objects made of steel. Wire ran from one to another.

Go to **34**.

44

'Oh, I was in my workroom,' said Uncle Quentin vaguely.

'Well, but where's that?' demanded Dick. 'Honestly, Uncle, we can't imagine where you hide yourself. We even went up the tower to see if you were in that funny glass room at the top.'

‘*What!*’ exploded his uncle, in a sudden, surprising fury. ‘You dared to go up there? You might have been in great danger. I’ve just finished an experiment, and all those wires in there were connected with it.’

‘Yes, we saw them lighting up,’ said Julian.

‘You’ve no business to come over here and interfere with my work,’ said Uncle Quentin, still looking furious. ‘Well, don’t you ever go into that tower again. I tell you, it’s dangerous.’

‘Uncle Quentin, you still haven’t told us yet where your workroom is,’ said Dick, who was quite determined to know. ‘We can’t imagine where you suddenly came from.’

Go to **48**.

45

A man and a boy were walking along the path. They were both well wrapped up in raincoats and wellies. The children took a look at them as they passed. The man was tall and well built, with shaggy eyebrows and a determined mouth. The boy was about sixteen, also tall and well-built. He was not a bad-looking boy, but he had rather a sulky expression.

'Good morning,' said the man, and nodded. 'Good morning,' chorused the children politely. The man looked them over keenly, then he and the boy went on.

'I wonder who they were?' said George. 'Mum didn't say there were any new people here.'

'Just walked over from the next village, I guess,' said Dick.

They went on for some way, till they came to a place where they could see down to the beach.

'Look,' said George suddenly. 'There's something down on the sand – something red.

I wonder what it is?'

'Perhaps we should go down and see,' suggested Dick.

'Shouldn't we go and tell the coastguard we've seen something strange?' asked Anne.

If you think they should go down to the beach, go to **50**.

If you think they should go and see the coastguard, go to **57**.

46

'There now,' said Aunt Fanny. 'I knew your father was somewhere about. I've heard that noise when I've been here before, but I couldn't make out where it came from.'

'It sounded almost as if it was underneath us,' said Dick, 'but it couldn't have been. This is really mysterious.'

No more noises came. They were just helping

themselves to doughnuts when Anne suddenly gave a squeal.

'Look! *There's* Uncle Quentin! Standing over there, near the tower! Where did he come from?'

Go to **40**.

47

'I really don't think it would be a good idea, George,' said Julian.

'Well, I'm not standing here while you two argue about it,' called Dick. 'I'm coming up!'

Dick and Anne were soon at the top.

'George! Are you coming up or not?' called Julian impatiently. 'If you don't come soon, it'll be time for lunch!'

'Yes!' shouted back George. 'I'm coming, and so is Timmy.'

A moment later George appeared at the top of the spiral staircase. Timmy went ahead of her into the room. It was a tight squeeze, with all of them in there together, and when they had admired the view Anne said, 'There's Aunt Fanny waving to us. Come on, let's go down.'

She began to go down the spiral staircase, but all of a sudden Timmy shot past her, making her lose her balance.

'Oh!' she gasped, as her feet slipped on the shiny steps.

Go to **37**.

48

'I told them you'd turn up, Quentin,' said his wife. 'You look a bit thin, dear. Have you been having regular meals? You know I left plenty of food for you.'

'Did you?' answered her husband. 'Well, I don't know if I've eaten or not. I don't worry about meals when I'm working. I'll have some of those sandwiches, though, if nobody else wants them.'

He began to devour the sandwiches, one after another, as if he were ravenous. Aunt Fanny watched him in distress.

'Oh, Quentin - you're starving. Do you think it would be a good idea if I came over here to look after you?' she said.

'Oh yes, Mum,' said George enthusiastically. 'We can manage on our own. You stay here with Dad!'

If you think Uncle Quentin should consider the idea, go to **54**.
If you think he shouldn't, go to **60**.

49

'We'd better go and check the cave,' said George firmly. 'It's a mistake to assume that because we can't *imagine* Dad doing something, he *can't* do it!'

'I suggest we go back to Aunt Fanny and have some lunch before we do anything else,' said Dick.

'You and your stomach!' said George scornfully. 'No, let's go and check the cave.'

Julian agreed with George, so they made their way past the castle to the other side of the island, where there was a cave they had once lived in. It could be entered with difficulty on the seaward side, or, alternatively, by dropping down a rope through a hole in the roof to the floor some way below.

They found the hole, half hidden in old heather. Julian felt about. The rope was still there.

'I'll slide down and have a look,' he said.

He went down the rope. It was knotted at intervals so that his feet found holding places, and he didn't slide down too quickly and scorch his hands.

Go to **39**.

50

'I think we ought to go down and find out what it is,' said George. 'It looks to me as though it might be a bit of sail from a yacht.'

'All right,' said Julian. 'Let's do as George says. Come on!'

They made their way down the steep path that ran down the cliff face to the beach. It was so narrow that they had to walk in single file, with Timmy slipping and sliding along behind them. The path was very slippery, and they hadn't gone very far before Dick lost his footing completely and fell flat on his back.

He wasn't hurt, but he felt a bit winded. He lay for a moment or two, trying to get his breath back.

'Get up, Dick!' said Julian. 'You'll be covered in mud if you lie there!'

'He's covered in mud anyway!' laughed Anne, as Dick struggled to his feet. 'Look at the back of his raincoat!'

The back of Dick's raincoat was muddy from

top to bottom!

'Aunt Fanny isn't going to be very pleased when she sees *that*,' said Anne. 'Your raincoat'll have to go to the cleaners. She'll never be able to brush that off!'

Go to **52**.

51

The next day was rainy. The four children put on raincoats and wellies, and went for a walk with Timmy. They never minded the weather.

'We forgot that Uncle Quentin wouldn't be able to signal to us if the sun wasn't out!' said Dick. 'Do you think he'll find another way to do it?'

'No,' said George. 'He just thinks we're making an awful fuss. We'll have to wait until ten-thirty tonight and see if he signals then.'

They walked up on to the top of the cliff. It was very windy indeed, and the rain stung their cheeks and made them gasp.

'I think we're the only people out walking this morning,' said George. 'Everyone else is keeping dry.'

'Well, you're wrong!' said Julian. 'There are two people coming towards us!'

Go to **45**.

52

Slowly they made their way down to the beach and walked over to where the piece of red cloth was lying. George picked it up and looked at it.

'I thought so,' she said. 'This is a piece of sail. It must have come from a yacht. I do hope that there isn't a boat out there in trouble – not in this awful weather.'

'Could it have come from one of the fishing boats?' asked Anne.

'No,' said Julian. 'If you remember, Anne, the

fishing boats all have engines. They don't use sails these days.'

Anne felt rather foolish. Of course none of the trawlers used sails.

'What do you think we should do, George?' asked Dick.

'We must go and see the coastguard,' said George firmly. 'He's the right person to deal with something like this.'

'Shouldn't we go to the police?' enquired Anne. 'Don't they deal with things like this sometimes?'

Go to **57**.

53

'I'm afraid he might get a shock if he brushes against any of these wires,' said Julian.

'All right,' said George. 'I'll leave him here.'

Soon the others were all at the top of the tower, admiring the view. They could see Timmy sitting on the ground waiting for them to reappear.

'There's Aunt Fanny waving to us,' said Dick. 'It must be lunchtime. Come on. There's nothing up here except these strange wires, and the view!'

They went back down the steep, narrow stairs, and walked over to where Aunt Fanny was sitting.

Go to **42**.

54

George's father looked startled. 'Stay here and look after me?' he repeated. 'What about the children, Fanny? Surely they need you at home?'

'Well, dear, they're all sensible and reliable,' replied his wife. 'I'm sure I could arrange for someone to come and look after the house and the cooking.'

'Oh, yes,' said George eagerly. 'We'll be perfectly all right on our own – it would be great fun!'

Uncle Quentin still looked doubtful. 'I don't

really need anyone to look after me. I'm perfectly all right on my own. Mind you, I suppose you could turn that little stone room into some kind of a kitchen . . .'

'I know!' said Dick, in great excitement. 'We could *all* come and live on the island! Then Aunt Fanny could look after all of us.'

'That would be fun,' said Anne. 'I loved it when we stayed here last time – it would be nice to do it again.'

It was all too much for Uncle Quentin. He had no desire to have the children and Aunt Fanny all living on the island with him.

Go to **60**.

55

'It's not my tin,' said the coastguard. 'It belongs to that boy next door. I told you he comes in to help me sometimes. He brought it in to help paint a little doll's house I made for his father.'

'Oh no,' said George in dismay. 'Do you think he'll be cross when he knows Timmy spilt it?'

'I don't think so,' replied the coastguard. 'He's a strange boy, though – quiet and a bit sulky.'

'I'll tell him I'm sorry if I meet him on the way back,' promised George, doing her best to clear up the mess.

'The weather's a bit brighter now,' said Dick. 'Can we please have a look through the telescope?'

'Yes, of course,' said the old man.

Everyone had a squint down the telescope. They could see Kirrin Island very clearly, but

there was no sign of Uncle Quentin.

'Well, thanks very much,' said Julian. 'If we're up here again, can we come and have another look, please?'

'You're welcome,' said the coastguard. 'Come along any time you want. I'll be pleased to see you.'

Go to **59**.

56

'No,' said Uncle Quentin firmly. 'I'm not going to tell you where I'm working, and that's that.'

'Could you at least signal to us every night and every morning, to show that you're all right?' asked Aunt Fanny.

Uncle Quentin frowned. 'Very well,' he said at last. 'I'll signal at half past ten, both morning and evening. Six torch flashes at night, and six flashes with a mirror in the morning. Now – I must get back to work.'

Despite George's protests that she wanted to spend more time on her precious island, her father firmly escorted them back to their boat. Julian shoved the boat off and leapt in himself. He cupped his hands round his mouth and shouted,

'Don't forget to signal, Uncle! We'll be watching out morning and evening!'

The boat slid away down the little inlet of water, and Uncle Quentin was lost to sight. Then round the low walls of rocks went the boat, and was soon out on the open sea.

'Ju, watch and see if you can make out where Uncle Quentin is, when we're round these rocks,' said Dick. 'See what direction he goes in.'

Julian looked for his uncle, but the rocks hid the cove from sight, and there was no sign of him at all.

'Why wouldn't he tell us where he's working?' said Dick. 'It must be somewhere we don't know about – it's a real mystery.'

Go to **51**.

57

If you have arrived from **52**, *score* 🐟 🐟.

'I think we should go and see the coastguard,' said Julian, so they all made their way along the narrow path up to the row of whitewashed cottages that stood on the cliff top. The coastguard lived in the first cottage, and the other two were let – usually to summer visitors.

The children knew the coastguard well. He was a large, cheerful man with a weather-beaten face.

'Hello, coastguard,' said Anne.

He looked up with a smile. 'Hello to you,' he replied. 'How nice to see you all again! Here for the holidays, are you?'

'That's right,' said George. 'My cousins are staying with me.'

'We've seen something down on the beach that we're a bit concerned about,' said Julian. 'It looks like a piece of sail from a yacht.'

'Oh, yes, I know all about that,' said the

coastguard. 'It fell overboard from a yacht a couple of days ago – the yacht owner rang me and told me that it was nothing to worry about. Thank you for mentioning it – that was very good of you.'

'What are you making?' asked Dick curiously, looking at the piece of wood the coastguard was holding.

'It's a little windmill – for my grandson,' the old man explained.

'Oh, it's *lovely*!' exclaimed Anne, taking it in her hands. 'Does the windmill part go round – look it does!'

'The man next door has bought quite a few of the toys I've made – says he wants to give them to his nephews and nieces.'

'Which man is that?' asked Julian.

Go to **63**.

58

‘It’s *my* island,’ said George proudly. ‘My very own.’

‘Really?’ said the boy politely. ‘Could you let me go over there one day?’

‘Well, not just now,’ said George. ‘You see, my father – he’s a scientist – is there at the moment, working on an experiment.’

‘Is that strange tower something to do with it?’ asked the boy, looking interested. ‘When will his experiment be finished?’

‘What’s that to do with you?’ asked Dick suddenly. The others stared at him in surprise. Dick had sounded rather rude, and that was not like him.

‘Nothing!’ said the boy hastily. ‘I only thought that if his work will soon be finished, your brother might take me over to his island.’

George was delighted at being taken for a boy.

‘Of *course* I’ll take you,’ she said. ‘It shouldn’t be too long before the experiment is finished.’

Go to **64**.

59

They said goodbye and went off, Timmy capering round them.

'Couldn't we see Kirrin Island well!' exclaimed Anne. 'I wish I could see where your father was, George. Wouldn't it be fun if we spotted him just coming out of his hiding-place?'

The four children had discussed this problem a good deal since they had left the island. It puzzled them very much indeed. How did it happen that George's father knew a hiding-place that they didn't know? It must be quite a big hiding-place, too, if he had got all his stuff for his experiments with him. According to George's mother, there had been quite a lot of this, as well as stores of food.

'He'll probably tell us when he's finished his experiments,' said Julian cheerfully. 'Then we'll all be able to go and explore it, wherever it is.'

As they made their way along the path, they could see someone quite a distance away, standing looking out to sea.

'I wonder if that's the boy we met earlier,' said Dick.

'No – I'm sure it's someone else,' said Anne. 'The boy we met isn't as tall as that.'

If you think it's the boy they met earlier, go to **65**.
If you think it's someone else, go to **71**.

60

If you've arrived from **54**, *score* 🐟.

'Oh, no!' George's father looked alarmed. 'Nobody is to stay here. I can't have my work interfered with. I'm working on an extremely important discovery.'

'Is it something that no one else knows about?' asked Anne, her eyes wide with admiration. How clever Uncle Quentin was!

'Well – I'm not sure about that,' said Uncle Quentin, taking two sandwiches at once. 'I have a feeling that somebody knows a bit more than I want them to know. But, no one can come over here unless they're shown the way through all those rocks that lie round the island. Only a few of the fishermen know that, and I've asked them not to bring anyone here. I think you're the only other person who knows the way, George.'

'Uncle Quentin, please tell us where your workroom is,' begged Dick, feeling that he could not wait a moment more to solve the mystery.

Go to **56**.

61

'Do many tourists mention the tower?' asked Julian.

'Not many,' answered Alf. 'Any that mention it seem to think that it's some kind of lighthouse. Oh - wait a minute now. There *was* one man seemed very interested in it - asked all sorts of questions, he did.'

'What sort of questions?' asked Dick excitedly.

'Oh, who owned the island, how long had the tower been built – all kinds of questions,' said Alf.

'What did the man look like?' asked Julian.

'Tall, he was,' replied Alf. 'Dark-haired, with a beard and glasses. Not a local man, I'm sure. Well, I must be getting back, or Mum'll be wondering what's happened to me. Nice to see you all!'

Alf walked off along the path, and the four children discussed what he had told them.

'Do you think we should tell Dad that someone is very interested in the island?' asked George.

Julian shook his head. 'No point,' he said. 'He'd just say it was nonsense – you know what he's like.'

'You're right, Julian,' said Dick, and the two girls agreed with him.

'Come on,' said Anne. 'We must get back, or Aunt Fanny will start to wonder where we are.'

They set off again, but had not gone very far when they saw someone else on the path ahead of them.

Go to **65**.

62

The next day dawned bright and sunny. The four tore down to breakfast, full of high spirits.

'What are you planning to do today?' asked Aunt Fanny, as they were finishing their meal.

'Well, first of all I think we'd better wait until Uncle Quentin has signalled at ten-thirty,' said Julian. 'You might need George to take you over to the island if he needs anything. We can decide what we're going to do after the signal has come.'

Promptly at half past ten Uncle Quentin signalled six flashes.

'That's OK, then,' said Dick. 'Right, shall we go for a swim?'

'A swim?' said Anne. 'The water will be much too cold. I vote we go and visit the old quarry. The primroses and violets should be out there by now.'

If you think they should go for a swim, go to **68**.
If you think they should visit the quarry, go to **73**.

63

'I've got some new neighbours in the cottage next door,' said the coastguard. 'Father and son, they are.'

'Oh, would they be the two we met, I wonder?' asked Dick. 'Both tall and well-built, and the man had shaggy eyebrows.'

'That's right,' said the coastguard, trimming a bit of his windmill. 'Mr Curton and his son. They came here some weeks ago. The boy's been ill, apparently, and had to take time off school - the doctor said he would benefit from the sea air. He seems like a nice boy - comes and helps with my models, occasionally. He enjoys looking through my telescope, too.'

'So do I,' said George. 'Can I have a go with it now? I'd like to see if I can spot Kirrin Island.'

'Well, you won't see much in this weather,' replied the old man. 'See that break in the clouds? If you wait till that moves this way, you should be able to see your island, George. That's a funny thing your father's built there, isn't it?'

'Yes, it is,' agreed George. 'Oh no – look what Timmy's done! He's upset that tin of paint. Bad boy, Timmy!'

Go to **55**.

64

A sound made them turn, and they saw the boy's father coming towards them. He nodded to the children.

'Making friends?' he asked amiably. 'That's right. Martin – my son – gets pretty lonely here. I hope you'll come and see us from time to time.'

Martin broke in. 'This boy says that island over there is his, and he's going to take me over to it when his father has finished his work there – and that won't be long.'

'Do you know the way through all those wicked

rocks?' asked the man. 'I wouldn't care to try it. I was talking to some of the fishermen the other day, and not one of them appeared to know the way!'

This was rather astonishing. Some of the fishermen *did* know it. Then the children remembered that the men had all been asked not to take anyone to the island while Uncle Quentin was at work there. It was clear that they had pretended not to know the way, out of loyalty to Uncle Quentin.

'Did you want to go to the island then?' asked Dick suddenly.

'Oh, no,' replied the man, 'but I thought it might interest Martin. I'm a very poor sailor. I never go on the sea if I can help it!'

Go to **69**.

65

If you've arrived from ***61****, score* ◯◯.

As they got closer, they could see that it was the boy they had met earlier. He turned as they came up to him and gave them a rather feeble smile.

'Hello!' he said. 'Been up to see the coastguard?'

'Yes, we have,' answered Julian.

'I'm so sorry,' said George, 'but my dog upset a tin of green paint, and the coastguard said it was yours. Can I pay you for it, please?'

'Don't worry,' said the boy. 'I don't mind. There wasn't much of it left anyway. That's a nice dog you've got.'

'Yes,' said George warmly. 'He's the best dog in the world. Do you like dogs?'

'Oh yes,' said the boy, but he made no move to pat Timmy. Timmy didn't run round the boy and sniff his legs the way he usually did when he met anyone new. He just stood beside George, his tail neither up nor down.

'That's an interesting-looking island,' said the boy, pointing to Kirrin Island. 'I wish I could go over to it.'

Go to **58**.

66

'I'll be careful,' promised Anne. 'I'll throw my basket down first, then I'll have both hands free to hang on.'

She flung the basket down, and it bounced all the way to the bottom of the quarry. The children climbed down to where they wanted to go – Anne to a large patch of primroses, George and the two boys to a place where they might find stone arrow-heads.

'Hello!' said a voice suddenly, from much lower down. The four stopped in surprise, and Timmy growled.

It was Martin Curton.

'Nice to see you,' said Julian. 'We've come to picnic here, and to search for stone weapons. What have you come for?'

'I want to see if I can find some weapons too,' said Martin.

'Come and join us,' invited Dick, who was trying to be friendly to make up for the way he had behaved the day before. Martin came over and began to scrape about. He had to use his hands, whereas the others had brought trowels with them.

Timmy had his head and shoulders down a rabbit hole. He was scrabbling violently, sending up heaps of earth behind him in a shower. A stone flew up and hit Julian. He rubbed his cheek. Then he inspected the stone that lay beside him, and gave a shout.

'Hey! Look at this!'

Go to **76**.

67

'Oh, come, Dick,' coaxed Anne.

'All right then,' said Dick rather sulkily, and they all set off back along the path to the row of whitewashed cottages.

Julian chatted to Martin's father as they walked. He was an interesting man, who had travelled abroad a great deal. Julian racked his brains to recall the man's name, which the coastguard had mentioned, and at last he remembered that it was Curton.

They all filed into the kitchen of the little cottage and took off their dripping boots and raincoats. Then they went through into the sitting-room, and Martin turned on the television. Mr Curton disappeared upstairs, saying he had one or two letters to write.

They had only been watching for a couple of minutes when there was a knock at the back door. Martin got up to see who it was.

Go to **72**.

68

‘What do you think, Julian?’ asked Dick. ‘Would you like to go for a swim?’

Julian looked out of the window at the sunny day.

‘Well, let’s go down and see what the water’s like,’ he said. ‘Are you coming, Anne?’

‘I’ll come down and sit on the beach and watch you all,’ said Anne. ‘I’m not going to swim, though.’

‘I think you’re all mad,’ said Aunt Fanny. ‘The water will be bitterly cold, you wait and see!’

The two boys and George ran upstairs and put their swimming things on under their jeans. Then they set off down to the beach, with Timmy running in front of them. He went straight down to the sea and started to splash around.

Dick threw off his clothes and ran down to the water’s edge.

Go to **75**.

69

‘Well, we’ve got to go,’ said Julian. ‘We’ve got to do some shopping for my aunt. Goodbye!’

‘Come and see us as soon as you can,’ said the man. ‘On a rainy day like today you could all watch our television.’

‘Oh, have you got a television?’ said George eagerly. She very seldom saw any television programmes, because her father refused to have a set in the house.

‘Yes, of course,’ laughed the man. ‘Why don’t you come back with us now and watch it for a while? I think there are one or two programmes on at this time of day that you might find quite interesting.’

‘Oh, yes!’ said George. ‘What do you think, Julian? Do you think Mum will mind?’

‘Aunt Fanny did say the shopping wasn’t very urgent,’ said Anne.

If you think they should go and watch television, go to **74**.

If you think they should go and do Aunt Fanny's shopping, go to **79**.

70

Later that evening Julian and Dick saw Uncle Quentin signal from the tower. George and Anne were already asleep, but the two boys lay with the curtains open, waiting for half past ten. Suddenly a light shone from the top of the tower. Julian began to count.

'One flash.' There was a pause. 'Two . . . three . . . four . . . five . . . six!'

There was a knock on the door, and then Aunt Fanny came in.

'Julian, did you see the flashes? I forgot to count them. Were there six?'

'Yes, Aunt Fanny!' answered Julian. 'I'd have come straight down to tell you if anything had been wrong. I'm sure Uncle Quentin's all right.'

'I wish I'd told him to do an extra flash to tell me

if he's had something to eat,' said his aunt. 'Well, goodnight, both of you. Sleep well!'

Go to **62**.

71

As they got nearer, they realised that the person standing on the cliff was not the boy they had met earlier, but Alf, the fisherman's son who used to look after Timmy in the days when George's father wouldn't allow her to keep the dog in the house.

'Hi, Alf!' said George. 'What are you doing up here?'

'I came up to bring the coastguard some fish that my father caught yesterday,' said Alf. 'He likes good fresh fish, does the coastguard. I just stopped to look over at your island, George. That's a funny-looking tower your father had built, isn't it?'

'Yes, it is,' agreed George. 'It'll be taken down when he's finished what he's doing.'

‘I know that whatever he’s doing is a secret,’ said Alf, ‘because he spoke to my father and all the other fishermen – asked them not to take any tourists round the island until the tower’s been taken down.’

‘Didn’t they mind?’ asked Dick, who knew that the fishermen made extra money by taking tourists on trips.

Alf shook his head. ‘All the fishermen like your father, George. They were happy to do what he asked.’

Go to **61**.

72

The children heard the sound of voices, and then Martin came back.

‘It’s the coastguard,’ he said. ‘It seems that George’s mother rang him to see if you were here.

She'd like you all to go home now for lunch. By the way,' he went on, 'which one of you is George?'

'I am,' said George, getting to her feet.

'The dog belongs to you, doesn't he?' went on Martin.

'Yes, he does,' replied George. Timmy, who had been sitting at her feet, got up when he saw them all getting ready to leave.

'Well, it's a pity we couldn't stay longer,' said Julian, 'but thank you for having us.'

'Come back another day,' invited Martin.

'Oh, yes,' said Anne. 'We'd like that.'

They climbed back into their raincoats and boots, and set off back down the cliff path to Kirrin Cottage.

Soon they were out of sight of the cottages.

Go to **86**.

73

‘Anne is right,’ said Aunt Fanny. ‘The sea will be terribly cold. Do you want to spend the rest of the holidays in bed with a chill?’

‘Well, let’s go and visit the old quarry, then,’ said Dick. ‘We might find one or two stone arrowheads that we could take back to school next term.’

‘I can pick some of the primroses and violets,’ said Anne.

‘Oh, yes – I’d like to have some to put round the house,’ said her aunt. ‘Shall I make some sandwiches for your lunch?’

‘Yes, please, Aunt Fanny,’ said Dick. ‘Do make plenty, won’t you?’

Aunt Fanny got a large picnic ready for them, and then the four children set off, with Timmy bounding in front of them.

Go to **78**.

Julian hesitated for a moment. His aunt had said that she would do the shopping herself after lunch if the children didn't have time. He felt sorry for Martin, too. He was obviously rather bored and lonely.

'No, I don't think Aunt Fanny will mind if we're a bit late,' he said. 'We'd love to come and watch your television for a while. Thank you.'

'Well, I don't want to,' said Dick, so rudely and abruptly that the others all stared at him.

'What on earth's the matter, Dick?' said Anne, who was standing beside him.

'I just don't want to go and watch television,' her brother replied. 'I can do that any time I want to at home. I'd rather do things outdoors while we're here at Kirrin. But don't let me stop you. I'll just go for a walk.'

'Oh, come with us, Dick,' said Julian. 'It won't be for long.'

If you think Dick should go with them, go to **67**.

If you think he should go off on his own, go to **82**.

75

The sea water broke over Dick's legs as he dashed into the waves. It was absolutely freezing! He danced up and down, trying to get warm. He couldn't face plunging into the water to swim. Julian and George came running down to join him.

'What's the water like, Dick?' asked George.

'It's *freezing*,' said Dick. 'Anne was right – it's much too cold. If I were you, I wouldn't bother even to paddle. I'm going to come out and get dressed.'

They pulled their clothes on again, and trudged back to Kirrin Cottage to ask Aunt Fanny to make them some sandwiches for a picnic lunch.

Go to **78**.

The others all came running to see what Julian had found.

'It's an arrowhead!' he exclaimed triumphantly. 'Thank you very much, Timmy!'

Martin didn't say much. He just looked at the arrowhead and turned away. Dick thought he was dull and rather boring. He wondered whether they should ask Martin to share their picnic. He didn't want to, but George certainly did!

'Are you having a picnic here too?' she asked.

Martin shook his head. 'I haven't brought any food with me,' he said.

'Well, you can share ours,' said George. 'We've got masses to eat.'

Martin looked pleased.

'Thank you very much,' he said. 'Will you come and watch my television this afternoon in return?'

'Oh, yes, please,' said George.

The boys found a stone shelf that stuck out a long way, and they decided to have their picnic on it. They were all very hungry. Martin shared their sandwiches, and became quite friendly over them.

'Best sandwiches I've ever tasted,' he said. 'I suppose your mother made them for you. I wish I had a mother. Mine died ages ago.'

There was a sympathetic silence. The four felt very sorry for Martin.

Go to **80**.

77

The rest of the day passed quickly. The weather cleared and the sun came out, and the air smelt of gorse and primroses and the salt of the sea. In the afternoon they went into town with Aunt Fanny, and stopped off to see their friend Alf, the fisherman's son.

After supper the children went out into the garden. They could see Kirrin Island and the tower very clearly. Suddenly they heard a faint rumbling sound, and the top of the tower blazed with a curious glare.

'Look!' exclaimed Julian in great excitement. 'That's what happened yesterday. Your father must be at work, George. I wonder what he's doing?'

Then there came a throbbing sound, almost like the noise of an aeroplane, and once more the glass top of the tower shone and blazed, as the wires became full of a strange power.

Aunt Fanny came out into the garden at that moment. 'Did you hear the noise?' she said. 'I suppose that was Quentin at work again. Oh dear, I hope he doesn't blow himself up one of these days!'

Go to **70**.

78

If you've arrived from **75**, *score* 🐟.

They went for a walk before making for the quarry, so that Timmy could stretch his legs. The quarry was only about a quarter of a mile from Kirrin Cottage. It was a strange place. At some time it had been quarried for stone, then left to itself. Now the sides were covered with small bushes and grass and plants of all kinds. Heather grew in the sandy places.

The sides were very steep, and since very few people ever visited the quarry, there were no paths to follow. It was like a huge rough bowl, irregular in places, and full of colour from the primroses, violets and cowslips that grew there in abundance.

'It's lovely!' exclaimed Anne, stopping at the top and looking down. 'I've never seen so many primroses before – and such big ones, too.'

'Be careful how you go, Anne,' warned Julian. 'The sides are very steep. If you lose your footing you'll roll right down to the bottom - and find yourself with a broken arm or leg!'

Go to **66**.

79

'I think we'd better go and get the shopping,' said Julian firmly. 'And Aunt Fanny won't like it if we're late for lunch. We'd love to come and watch your television another day, if we could.'

'Yes, of course,' said the man. 'Well - I'm very pleased to have met you. My name's Curton, by the way.'

He shook hands with Julian, Anne and George, but Dick pretended not to see his outstretched hand, and started to walk away. Mr Curton just gave a laugh, and went off towards the cottages on the cliff top, followed by Martin.

Go to **86**.

'I saw your father flashing his signals last night,' said Martin, munching a bun.

Dick looked up at once. 'How do you know he was signalling?' he asked. 'Who told you?'

'Nobody,' answered Martin. 'I saw the six flashes, and I thought it must be George's father.' He looked surprised at Dick's sharp tone. Julian gave Dick a nudge, to warn him not to go off the deep end again.

George scowled at Dick. 'I suppose you saw my father signalling this morning, too,' she said to Martin. 'He heliographs with a mirror at half past ten in the morning, and flashes a lantern at the same time at night, to show that he's all right.'

Now it was Dick's turn to scowl at George. Why give away all this information? It wasn't necessary.

Timmy was sitting on the warm stone with the others. He was funny with Martin. He took absolutely no notice of him at all! Martin ignored Timmy, too. He didn't talk to him, or pat him. It was all rather odd. After all, George was talking in a friendly way to Martin, and the others had shared their food with him – and Timmy behaved as if Martin simply wasn't there!

Anne was just about to remark on Timmy's odd behaviour when the big dog yawned, shook himself, and leapt down from the rock. He disappeared under the shelf of rock, and there came the sound of digging. A shower of stones and soil flew into the air. The children lay back on the stone, feeling sleepy. They talked for some minutes, then Anne felt her eyes closing. She was

awakened by George's voice.

'Where's Timmy? Timmy! Timmy! Come here! Where have you got to?'

No Timmy appeared. George stood up on the platform of rock and looked round the quarry.

'Oh, no!' she said to herself. 'Now I'll have to go and look for him. I wonder which way he went? There are some rabbit holes over there – he might have got stuck in one of them that I can't see, or he might be exploring under this rock. Which way shall I go?'

If you think George should search by the rabbit holes, go to **87**.

If you think she should look under the rock, go to **93**.

81

When she reached the clump of gorse George dropped on to her hands and knees, thinking she would be safer like that. Then she crawled round to the far side of the gorse to look for more rabbit holes, but there were none there.

'Bother!' exclaimed George crossly. 'Where *has* Timmy gone?'

She stood up very carefully and looked round. She called Timmy's name once or twice, but there was still no sign of him. George looked over to the platform of rock on which the others were sleeping. She giggled, thinking they looked rather funny, especially Dick and Anne, who had both gone to sleep with their mouths open!

She dropped to her hands and knees again and began to work her way round the gorse bush and back towards the rock.

Go to **90**.

82

Dick shook his head. 'No, thank you,' he said. 'I'd rather go off on my own.' He turned on his heel and set off down the path towards Kirrin.

The others walked back to the row of whitewashed cottages with Martin and his father, but just as they got there the coastguard came out of his door and hailed them.

'Your mother just rang me to see if you were here,' he said. 'She wants you to get back for lunch now.'

'*Bother!*' said George. 'Oh, well, it was nice of you to ask us to watch your television. Could we come another day?'

'Yes, of course,' said Martin's father, shaking hands with them all. 'My name's Curton, by the way.'

The children said goodbye to Martin and made their way back down the cliff path towards Kirrin Cottage. They hadn't gone very far before they caught up with Dick, who was plodding along with his head down and his hands in his pockets.

'Hello!' he exclaimed. 'I thought you were all watching television.'

Anne explained about the message from Aunt Fanny.

'Just as well we've all got to get back,' muttered Dick.

Go to **86**.

83

They all climbed the steep side of the quarry and made their way towards the coastguard's cottage. He was out in the garden, and he waved to them as they went past.

They went through the gate of the next door cottage, and Martin pushed the door open. His father was sitting by the window, reading the paper. He got up with a broad, welcoming smile.

'Well, how nice to see you! Come in. Yes, bring the dog in as well. I like dogs.'

The children all shook hands politely, and Martin explained about the television programme.

'What a good idea,' said Mr Curton, still beaming.

The four looked round the room. There was a large television set at the far end of the room – and something else that made the boys stare with interest.

'Look at that!' exclaimed Julian. 'You've got a transmitting set, as well as a receiver.'

'Yes,' said Mr Curton. 'It's a hobby of mine. I made that set.'

'What's a transmitting set?' asked Anne. 'I've never heard of one before.'

'It's like the sort of thing that police cars have,' explained Dick. 'You can send messages to other people, as well as receive them.'

Martin turned the television on.

'How about something to drink?' offered Mr Curton. 'Anne, would you give me a hand?'

They returned from the kitchen with a large jug of orange squash and some glasses, then the children all settled down to watch the programme. Everyone enjoyed it. Just as it was finishing the coastguard came to the door.

'Your ma just rang, George,' he said. 'She wants

you all to go home for tea.'

'Would you like to stay and have tea with us?' asked Mr Curton.

If you think they should go home for tea, go to **92**.
If you think they should stay and have tea, go to **99**.

84

George pushed at the earth with her trowel, and to her relief felt it move a little. She dug hard, and soon had shifted enough earth to give her room to crawl on.

'TIMMY!' she shouted again. 'Where are you?'

From somewhere deep in the quarryside there came a faint whine. George felt thankful. So Timmy *was* there, after all. She crawled a bit further. Suddenly the tunnel became high and wide, and she realised that she must be in a passage. Then she heard the sound of pattering feet, and Timmy pressed affectionately against her legs, whining.

'Oh, Timmy – you gave me such a fright!' said George.

'Woof,' said Timmy, and pulled at George's jeans to make her go back to the daylight.

'All right,' said George. 'I'm coming!'

She made her way back to the shelf of rock, and crawled thankfully out into the fresh air, followed by Timmy.

Go to **89**.

85

'I had to stop you telling Martin's father all about the island, George!' explained Dick. 'I thought he seemed far too interested in it – and in Uncle Quentin's research.'

'I know why he asked all those questions,' said Anne unexpectedly.

The others looked at her in surprise.

'What do you mean?' asked Julian.

'Do you remember that I went out to the kitchen to help Mr Curton bring in the orange squash?' said Anne.

The others all nodded.

'Well, he mentioned that he had to telephone his newspaper after tea,' went on Anne. 'He's a journalist! He said something about writing a feature on Kirrin Island and the village and everything – what a fantastic place this is for a holiday.'

'Oh, I *see*!' exclaimed Dick.

Julian looked at his watch. 'It's time we were getting back,' he said. 'Come on!'

Go to **94**.

86

If you've arrived from **82**, *score* 🐟.

If you've arrived from **72**, *score* 🐟 🐟.

'Dick!' exploded George. 'What on earth made

you behave like that? You were really rude to Mr Curton.'

'I just felt suspicious, that's all,' said Dick. 'That boy seemed so interested in the island and in your father's work.'

'Why shouldn't he be?' demanded George. 'Everyone in the village is interested. They all know about the tower. All Martin wanted to know was when he could go to my island – that's why he asked when my father's work would be finished. I liked him.'

'You only liked him because he was silly enough to think you were a boy,' retorted Dick. 'Pretty odd-looking sort of boy, if you ask me!'

George flared up at once. 'Don't be mean! I *do* look like a boy – everyone says so!'

Anne looked rather worried. She was afraid George would really go off the deep end. Still, it was strange of Dick to be so rude. And she suddenly remembered that Timmy hadn't seemed to like Martin either.

'Well, we can always go back and watch television

another day,' said Julian calmly, 'but perhaps it would be best not to mention your father's work at all, George – just to be on the safe side!'

Go to **77**.

87

George stood still and listened for a minute. There was absolutely no sound. The others all seemed to have dozed off. She called Timmy once or twice, but no black and white dog came bounding towards her.

'I'll go and look over by those rabbit holes,' said George to herself. 'I expect that's where he is.'

She began to pick her way carefully across the side of the quarry. There were no paths, and though some places were covered in rough grass and flowers, there were other spots that were a mass of loose stones, and George knew that she would have to be careful crossing them. It would be easy to slip and go crashing to the bottom of the quarry in a shower of stones.

The rabbit holes George had spotted were not very far away from the rock they had all been sitting on, but it took her quite a long time to work her way over to them. There were two or three, just in front of one of the clumps of gorse that grew here and there. George thought there might be more hidden by the gorse.

Go to **81**.

88

'How about playing a game of some sort?' suggested Dick.

George looked out of the window.

'It's a fantastic evening,' she said. 'Why don't we go out for a walk?'

'George!' exclaimed Dick. 'We've walked miles already today.'

'Well, I'd like to go out again,' said Anne. 'What do you think, Julian?'

'I vote we go out,' replied her brother. 'It's too nice an evening to stay in! Is that all right, Aunt Fanny?'

'Oh yes,' said his aunt, 'but don't stay out too long, will you?'

'Let's walk down to the beach,' said George, as they got up from the table and went to find their anoraks.

As they walked along the road towards the beach, they met Mr Curton and Martin.

'Hello!' said Mr Curton. 'How nice to see you again so soon. I was just admiring the island, George. It looks beautiful in the evening light.'

George was pleased.

'Yes,' she said. '*I* always think that. I wish my father hadn't chosen this particular time to work on my island. I'd planned to go and stay there.'

Go to **95**.

89

If you've arrived from **97**, *score* 🐟.

By this time all the others were awake, and George told them what had happened.

'There's a passage behind the entrance to the hole under the rock,' she said. 'I couldn't see where it went, of course, because it was dark. Timmy was a long way in. Shall we explore it?'

Dick shook his head. 'Not today,' he said, looking at Julian, and Julian guessed that Dick didn't want Martin to share the secret. Julian nodded.

'No, let's not explore today,' he said. 'Anyway, it may be nothing – just an old tunnel made by the quarrymen.'

Martin was listening with great interest. He went and looked into the hole. 'I wish we *could* explore,' he said. 'Maybe we could plan to meet again with torches and see if there really is a passage there.'

Julian looked at his watch. 'Nearly two o'clock. Well, Martin, if we're going to see that half past two programme on your television, we'd better be going.'

Go to **83**.

90

George moved carefully across a large patch of grass to the stony area that lay just beside the big rock. She stepped on to it cautiously, but had only taken a couple of steps when loose stones began to slide away under her feet! She tried to steady herself, but her feet were slipping sideways. The next moment she had fallen over, and was sliding down the side of the quarry in a shower of stones!

Fortunately there was a large clump of gorse a little way below, and it broke George's fall. A shower of stones bumped and crashed its way down to the bottom.

George lay against the gorse, trying to get her breath back. It was rather prickly stuff to lean on, but she was feeling quite shaken by her fall and was glad to lie still for a moment. She looked up towards the rock to see if the noise of the rockfall had woken any of the others, and spotted something that made her sit up.

Slowly and carefully she climbed back up the side of the quarry to the rock.

Go to **93**.

91

George pushed at the earth with her trowel, but it felt pretty solid. A feeling of panic started to rise inside her. If Timmy was in the tunnel, he might well be trapped on the other side of the earth fall.

There was no room in the passage for her to turn round, so she crawled out backwards. Soon she was back in the fresh air. Standing up, she brushed the earth off her jeans and climbed back on to the rock where her cousins and Martin were lying. The others were all still asleep, but Julian was sitting up, looking a bit worried.

'There you are, George,' he said. 'Did you find Timmy?'

'No,' said George. 'There's quite a big passage – big enough for me to crawl along on my hands and knees – but it's blocked by an earth fall. Timmy might be trapped on the other side of it!'

Julian heard the slight note of panic in George's voice.

'Come on,' he said. 'Let's go back and see if we can find him. He may not be in there at all, you know. Did you hear him?'

George shook her head. 'I'm fairly sure he's in there somewhere, though,' she said.

Go to **97**.

92

The children looked at each other, then Julian spoke.

'It's very kind of you to ask us to stay, Mr Curton,' he said, 'but my aunt has been on her own all day, and I think we should go home for tea.'

'Very well,' said Mr Curton. 'But come and watch the television again, won't you? I'd like to see you all.'

The children said goodbye and trooped out.

'I'm starving!' said Dick, as they walked down the cliff path towards Kirrin. 'Let's hurry!'

'You're always starving,' said George with a grin.

Soon they were back at Kirrin Cottage. Aunt Fanny was delighted with the primroses and violets that Anne had picked in the old quarry.

'They'll look very nice on that table in the hall,' she said. 'Thank you, Anne.'

After tea they sat around the dining-room table, discussing what to do next.

Go to **88**.

93

If you've arrived from **90**, *score* 🐟🐟🐟.

Peering under the rock, George could see a large hole, scattered with stones that Timmy must have loosened in his digging.

'Surely he hasn't found a rabbit hole at last that's big enough for him to go down!' said George to herself. 'TIMMY! Where are you?'

Not a bark, not a whine came from the hole. George wriggled closer and peered down the burrow. Timmy had certainly made it very big.

Julian had woken up by now, and called down to ask George what she was doing. She explained what had happened, and then asked Julian to throw down his trowel so that she could make the hole bigger.

The trowel landed by her foot. She started to dig, and soon got very hot. Soon she had made the hole big enough to get through. She was surprised to find quite a large passage, once she had made the entrance big enough to take her. She could crawl along it on hands and knees!

'I wonder if this is just an animal's burrow – or if it really leads somewhere,' George thought as she crawled along. She had to feel along the floor with her hands, as it was pitch black in the tunnel. Suddenly she bumped her head on something. Feeling around, she guessed it was a place where the earth had fallen in, blocking the tunnel. George sat back on her heels and wondered what to do. Should she try and break through the earth and go on, or should she go back and ask for help?

If you think George should go on, go to **84**.
If you think she should go back, go to **91**.

94

They were all very tired by the time they got back to Kirrin Cottage, and George and Anne were happy to go straight to bed. Dick and Julian stayed up for a while, talking over the day's events.

'Don't forget to watch for Uncle Quentin's signal,' Julian reminded his aunt as they were about to go upstairs to bed.

'No, I won't!' she laughed. She was about to say something else when suddenly they heard a muffled bark from upstairs.

'What's the matter with Timmy, I wonder?' said Dick. Just as he spoke, there was a loud knock at the back door.

'Whoever can that be, at this time in the evening?' said Julian. 'Shall I go, Aunt Fanny?'

'No, dear,' said his aunt. 'I expect it's Mrs Williams from the village with some shopping I left in the baker's this morning. She said she'd drop it in on her way back from her daughter's house.'

'I'll come with you,' said Julian. 'Just in case.'

They hurried through the kitchen to the back door.

If you think it's Mrs Williams, go to **101**.
If you think it's someone else, go to **107**.

95

If you've arrived from **88**, *score* ○.

'I suppose you know every inch of it?' said Mr Curton.

'Oh yes!' replied George. 'We all do. There are dungeons under the castle, you know. We found some gold ingots there once.'

'Yes – I remember reading about that,' said Mr Curton. 'That must have been exciting. Isn't there an old well, too?'

'Yes,' answered Anne. 'There's also a cave where we lived once. It's got an entrance through its roof, as well as from the sea.'

'I suppose your father is carrying out his experiments in the dungeons, is he?' said Mr Curton.

'No, we don't . . .' began George, when she got a very sharp kick on the ankle from Dick. She screwed up her face in pain.

'What were you going to say?' asked Mr Curton, taken aback.

'Er – I was just going to say that – er – er – we don't know which place my father has chosen.'

Dick suddenly broke into the conversation.

'It's time we were going!' he said. 'Come on, all of you.'

Mr Curton and Martin both looked rather surprised that Dick was in such a hurry, but they said goodbye, and the four children set off.

'What on *earth* did you kick me for, Dick?' asked George. 'It really hurt!'

Go to **85**.

96

Julian noticed that the man seemed to be trying to see further into the kitchen. There was something strange about him – something rather sinister. Julian wanted to get rid of him as quickly as possible.

'My aunt has told you she hasn't got a room to let,' he said. 'Now please go away!'

The man didn't move.

'I understand that your husband is not at home at the moment,' he said.

'How do you know that my husband is away?' demanded Aunt Fanny angrily.

'Oh – er – the person who told me about the room,' the man replied. 'But, I seem to have made a mistake. I'm sorry if I bothered you. Good evening!'

Aunt Fanny closed the back door and locked it.

'Come into the sitting-room, Julian,' she said. 'I want to talk to you.'

Go to **100**.

97

Julian and George slid down off the slab of rock and peered into the tunnel.

'TIMMY!' shouted George at the top of her voice. 'Timmy, are you there?'

To George's joy, there was a muffled bark. She called again, and a minute or two later Timmy wriggled out into the sunshine. He was covered with earth, but apart from that seemed none the worse for his experience. He shook himself hard, and earth flew all over George and Julian.

'Thank you very much, Timmy!' said Julian with a laugh.

George was so relieved to see Timmy that she made a huge fuss of him, instead of scolding him for disappearing like that.

Go to **89**.

'Seven!' exclaimed Julian. Then another came. Eight. Nine. Ten. Eleven. Twelve.

'How strange!' said Julian. 'Why twelve flashes? Look – there are more coming!'

Another six flashes came from the tower, then nothing more. Julian wished that he had a telescope so that he could see right into the tower. He sat and thought for a moment, feeling very puzzled. Then the other three burst into the room.

'Julian! Dad flashed eighteen times instead of six! What do you think he means by it?' asked George.

'I expect he wants to let us know that he needs something,' said Julian. 'When Aunt Fanny gets back we'd better all go over to the island and see what he wants – more food, I expect.'

'Perhaps we ought to go up to the coastguard's cottage right away and look through his telescope,' suggested Dick. 'To see if we can make out anything strange or different on the island.'

If you think they should wait for Aunt Fanny, go to **106**.

If you think they should go up to the coastguard's cottage, go to **112**.

99

'Well, that's very kind of you,' said Julian. 'We would like to stay.'

'I'll ring your aunt and tell her that you're staying here,' said Mr Curton. 'I'll give her my number so that she doesn't have to ring the coastguard every time she wants to leave a message for you. After all, I hope you'll visit us often.'

Mr Curton rang Aunt Fanny. Yes, it was quite all right for them to stay, but they mustn't be too late back. So they settled down to a very good tea. Martin was not very talkative, but Mr Curton made up for it. He laughed and joked and was altogether very good company.

The talk came round to Kirrin island. Mr Curton

said how beautiful it looked each evening. George was pleased.

'Yes,' she said. '*I* always think that. I wish my father hadn't chosen this particular time to work on my island. I'd planned to go and stay there.'

Go to **95**.

100

'That was all very strange,' said Julian as they sat down.

'I know,' replied his aunt. 'Julian, he must have made up all that business about me having a room to let! Everyone in Kirrin knows that I've never let rooms to visitors in all the years we've lived here.'

'Yes, and how did he know that Uncle Quentin was away?' said the boy.

'Well, I suppose it's possible that somebody in Kirrin might have told him *that*,' said Aunt Fanny.

'Everyone knows Quentin's over on the island, don't they?'

'That's true,' agreed Julian. 'Are you going to tell Uncle Quentin about the man when we next see him?'

'No, dear, I don't think so,' she answered. 'It would worry him. I expect there's some perfectly simple explanation for the whole thing, so don't worry about it. Off you go to bed now. I won't forget to watch for your uncle's signal. Good night, dear.'

'Good night, Aunt Fanny,' Julian replied, and went up to bed.

Go to **104**.

101

Aunt Fanny opened the door. A pleasant-faced woman was standing there.

'Hello, Mrs Williams,' said Aunt Fanny. 'Is that my shopping?'

Mrs Williams handed Aunt Fanny two carrier bags.

'It's very kind of you to bring it up for me,' went on Aunt Fanny. 'I can't think how I managed to leave it in the baker's like that – I must have been dreaming! Thank you very much.'

'That's quite all right,' said Mrs Williams. 'I was passing the house on my way home, so it was no trouble. Good evening!'

'Good evening,' replied Aunt Fanny, and closed the door. She turned to Julian.

'Well now, it's getting late,' she said. 'You'd better go to bed. I'll watch for your uncle's signal at half past ten. Good night.'

'Good night, Aunt Fanny,' said Julian, and went up to bed.

Go to **104**.

102

George directed the telescope towards the island and focused on the tower. She could see it very clearly. There was no one in the little room at the top. The sun glittered on the wires and the glass, and it all looked perfectly normal.

She scanned the rest of the island, but it looked calm and peaceful in the spring sunshine.

'Can I have a look, please?' said Dick, and George moved away. Though they all took it in turns to scan Kirrin Island, none of them could see anything at all odd, or strange, or out of place.

'Well, everything certainly *looks* OK,' said Julian finally. 'We'd better get back to Kirrin Cottage. Thank you very much, coastguard.'

'That's all right,' said the coastguard. 'Nice to see you all!'

When the children got back to Kirrin Cottage, their note was lying on the hall table.

'Mum's still out,' said George.

Go to **106**.

103

‘Let’s talk about this calmly for a moment,’ said Aunt Fanny. ‘Now, Quentin, have you searched the island to see if there are any other signs that somebody else might be here?’

‘Of course not,’ answered her husband crossly. ‘I’ve been much too busy for that sort of thing!’

‘Well, in that case I think we should do as Julian suggests,’ said Aunt Fanny.

‘Oh, good!’ cried George. ‘Dick, will you come with me?’

‘Hang on, George!’ said Julian with a grin. ‘Let’s decide where we’re going to look first.’

‘There aren’t that many places to look,’ snapped his cousin. ‘There’s only the castle, really. Oh – what about the big cave, though? I’d forgotten that.’

‘Right,’ said Julian. ‘George, you come with me and we’ll go and look at the cave. Dick and Anne, you stay here and search every corner of the castle. What about you and Aunt Fanny, Uncle Quentin?'

'We'll sit quietly and drink our coffee,' said Aunt Fanny with a smile. 'I don't think you need our help.'

If you want to go with Julian and George, go to **108**.
If you want to go with Dick and Anne, go to **117**.

104

If you've arrived from **100**, *score* 🐟 🐟.

Julian lay in bed and looked out of the window towards Kirrin Island. The six flashes came at half past ten precisely. Julian counted them before dropping off to sleep.

Some time later he was woken by a throbbing noise. He sat up and looked out of the window, expecting to see the top of the tower ablaze with light, as it sometimes was when his uncle conducted

an experiment, but nothing happened. There was no flare of light, and Julian lay down again and went back to sleep.

'I saw Uncle Quentin's signals last night, Aunt Fanny,' he said next morning. 'Did you?'

'Yes,' said his aunt. 'Julian, do you think you could watch for them this morning? I have to go and see the vicar about something, and I don't believe I shall be able to see the tower from the vicarage.'

'Yes, of course I will, Aunt Fanny.' said Julian. 'What's the time now? Half past nine. I'll write some letters sitting by the window in my room, and I'll be able to see the signals from there.'

Aunt Fanny set off for the vicarage, and Julian went upstairs to write his letters. At half past ten he looked at the top of the tower. Ah – there was the first signal, blazing brightly as the sun caught the mirror held by his uncle in the tower.

'One flash,' counted Julian. 'Two – three – four – five – six. He's all right.'

He was just about to turn away when another flash caught his eye.

Go to **98**.

105

George looked at her mother.

'Mum! Do tell Dad that I must stay here with Timmy!'

'No, George,' replied her mother. 'Your father is right. Timmy must stay behind – and I won't allow you stay with him. I can't have both of you exposed to danger. It's bad enough worrying about your father as it is.' Aunt Fanny suddenly had an inspiration. 'Now George, if you could ask Timmy if he minded being left behind to guard your father, what do you think he would say? You know he would agree, even though he would miss you.'

George looked at Timmy, and he looked back at her, wagging his tail. Then he did an extraordinary thing – he got up, walked over to George's father, and lay down beside him, looking at George as if to say, 'There you are! Now you know what *I* think is right.'

'You see?' said her mother. 'He agrees with me. You've always said that Timmy was a good dog, and this proves it. You should be proud of him.'

Go to **115**.

106

If you've arrived from **102**, *score* 🐟 🐟.

When Aunt Fanny came home they told her what had happened.

'We must definitely go over to the island this morning,' she said. 'I'll go and pack plenty of food for your uncle. George, is your boat ready?'

'Yes, Mum,' said George. 'Alf told me the other day that he would have it ready for me to use whenever I want to.'

Aunt Fanny packed some food, and they set off to Kirrin Island in George's boat.

As they rounded the low wall of rocks and came into the little cove, they saw Uncle Quentin waiting for them. He helped to pull in the boat when it ran gently on to the sand.

'We saw your treble signal,' said Aunt Fanny. 'Did you want something, Quentin?'

'Yes, I did,' said Uncle Quentin. 'What's that you've got in your basket, Fanny? More of those delicious sandwiches? Good, I'll have some!'

'Oh Quentin - haven't you been having proper meals *again*?' said Aunt Fanny. 'Well - we'd better sit down and have something to eat now.'

Go to **110**.

107

Aunt Fanny opened the door. There was a man standing there. He was tall and dark, with a beard and glasses.

'Good evening,' he said. 'I'm sorry to bother you, but I understood from someone in the village that you had a room to let for a couple of weeks, and I wondered if I might see it?'

Aunt Fanny stared at the man in surprise.

'A room to let! Certainly not!' she said. 'I can't think who can have told you such a thing!'

'The person I spoke to seemed very certain,' answered the man. 'This *is* Kirrin Cottage, isn't it?'

'Yes, it is,' said Aunt Fanny, 'but I can only repeat, I don't have a room to let!'

'What's the matter, Aunt Fanny?' said Julian. 'Can I help?'

Aunt Fanny turned to him in relief.

'This gentleman says he was told by someone in the village that I had a room to let,' she explained. 'I can't seem to make him understand that I don't let rooms to holiday visitors!'

Go to **96**.

108

Julian and George set off towards the cave, with Timmy bounding in front of them. As they walked, they kept their eyes open for any more clues that there might be someone else on the island, but they didn't find anything.

Soon they were on the cliff top, looking out at the open sea. It was blue and sparkling in the spring sunshine.

'Come on, George,' said Julian, preparing to lower himself down into the cave through a hole in the cliff top. The old rope that they had used before was still hanging there. It was knotted at intervals, and both of them slid down swiftly on to the fine white sand on the cave floor. Timmy had to stay up on the cliff top. He could only get into the cave by scrambling over the rocks at low tide.

It was very quickly obvious that nobody had been using the cave as a hiding-place. The only thing in it was an old box that they had left behind themselves. There was no sign that any stranger had been there.

'Well,' said George, when they had had a good look round. 'There's nothing odd here! Come on, we'd better go back to the others.'

They made their way back across the cliff to where Uncle Quentin and Aunt Fanny were sitting enjoying the sunshine and drinking coffee.

Go to **116**.

109

Uncle Quentin and Aunt Fanny were sitting in the sun, enjoying a cup of coffee.

'Uncle Quentin, can you please give us a torch?' asked Dick. 'We need one to search the darker bits of the castle.'

'Are you sure you can't manage without one?' replied his uncle crossly. 'I really don't want to have to go and get one just at the moment.'

'It would really help to have a torch,' said Anne.

'Oh, very well,' said Uncle Quentin. 'You two stay here with your aunt. *Don't* follow me, do you understand?'

'Yes, Uncle,' said Dick and Anne together. Dick had secretly hoped that he might be able to go with Uncle Quentin and find out exactly where he was working!

Uncle Quentin disappeared into the castle. He was gone about ten minutes, and then reappeared with a torch in his hand.

'Here you are, then,' he said.

Dick and Anne searched every corner of the castle as thoroughly as they could. Just as Dick was about to give up in disgust, he heard Anne give a shout.

'Dick! Come and see what I've found!'

Go to **113**.

110

Aunt Fanny began to unpack the food. The children helped her set it out on the beach.

'Well, dear, how is your work getting on?' asked Aunt Fanny, watching her husband devour one sandwich after another. She began to wonder if he had had anything to eat since she had left him two days ago.

'Oh, very well indeed,' said her husband. 'Couldn't be better – just got to a most tricky and interesting bit. I'll have another sandwich, please.'

'Why did you signal eighteen times, Uncle Quentin?' asked Anne.

'Ah, well – it's difficult to explain, really,' said her uncle. 'The fact is – I can't help feeling there's somebody on this island besides myself!'

Go to **114**.

111

'But, Dad - Timmy and I are never separated,' she said at last, in a pleading voice. 'I do see that you want him to guard you - and you *can* have him - but I'll have to stay here too!'

'Oh, no!' said her father at once. 'You can't possibly stay, George. That's out of the question. As for never being separated from Timmy, surely you wouldn't mind that for once, if it was to ensure my safety?'

George swallowed hard. This was the most difficult decision she had ever had to make in her life. Leave Timmy behind on the island - where there was some unknown, hidden enemy, who might harm him!

Yet there was her father, too - he might be in danger if there was no one to guard him.

'I'll *have* to stay here, Dad,' she said. 'I can't leave Timmy behind. It's no good.'

Her father began to lose his temper. He was like George - he wanted his own way, and if he didn't get it he was going to make a fuss!

'If I'd asked Julian or Dick or Anne this same thing, and they'd had a dog, they would all have said yes, at once!' he raged. 'You, George, you must always make things difficult if you can! You and that dog – anyone would think he was worth a thousand pounds!'

'He's worth more than that to me,' said George, her voice trembling. Timmy crept nearer to her and pushed his nose into her hand. She held his collar as if she would not let him go for a moment.

Go to **105**.

112

'That's a good idea, Dick,' said Julian. 'We'll do that before Aunt Fanny comes back.'

'Do you think there's something wrong with Uncle Quentin?' said Anne, sounding rather scared.

'No, I don't think so,' said Julian reassuringly.

'The most likely explanation is that he wants more food, but we'll soon see.'

'Do you think that one of us ought to stay here and tell Aunt Fanny what's happened?' asked Anne. 'Or shall we leave her a note?'

'Leave her a note,' said George at once. 'I don't think she'll be back for ages, because the vicar's wife is very talkative, so there's no point one of us staying here.'

She quickly scribbled a note for her mother, and then they all set off up to the coastguard's cottage. He was in the garden, as usual.

'Good morning,' he said cheerfully. 'Come to look through my telescope again?'

'Yes, please,' said George, and they all went into the cottage.

Go to **102**.

113

Dick raced over to where Anne was standing, at the entrance to the little room. She held out her hand to Dick. In it was a small piece of newspaper.

'Look!' she said. 'The date is on the top!'

'The 16th!' exclaimed Dick. 'Why – that was the day before yesterday. There *is* someone else here! Come on, let's go and show Uncle Quentin.'

When Dick and Anne got back to the cove, Julian and George had returned.

'There was nothing in the cave,' said Julian. 'Did you two find anything?'

'Yes!' cried Anne triumphantly, and showed them the piece of newspaper.

'Well, I don't think there can be any doubt about it now,' said Uncle Quentin. 'There *must* be somebody else here.'

Go to **119**.

'Quentin! What in the world do you mean?' cried Aunt Fanny in alarm. She looked over her shoulder as if she half expected to see somebody there. All the children stared at Uncle Quentin in amazement.

He took another sandwich. 'Yes, I know it sounds mad. Nobody else could possibly have got here, but I *know* there's someone!'

'Oh, don't, Uncle!' said Anne with a shiver. 'It sounds horrid. You're all alone at night, too!'

'That's just it,' replied her uncle. 'I would mind if I *was* all alone at night. What worries me is that I don't think I am!'

'Uncle, what makes you think there's somebody here?' asked Julian.

'Well, when I finished the experiment I was doing last night – at about half past three in the morning, I think – it was still pitch dark, of course,' replied Uncle Quentin. 'I came into the open for a breath of fresh air, and I swear I heard someone cough – twice!'

'Good gracious!' exclaimed Aunt Fanny. 'But you might have been mistaken, Quentin. After all, you were probably very tired.'

'Yes, I know,' said her husband. 'But, I couldn't make a mistake about *this*, could I?'

He held out his hand. On his palm was a cigarette end, still crisp and fresh.

'I don't smoke cigarettes, and nor do you, Fanny,' went on Uncle Quentin. 'We're the only people apart from the children who've been on the island recently. Who smoked that cigarette, and, since none of the fishermen would bring anyone over here, how did he get here?'

They all looked at each other in dismay. Then Julian got to his feet.

'I think it would be a good idea if we searched the island thoroughly,' he said. 'Come on, let's split up and have a good look round.'

'Wait a moment,' said Aunt Fanny. 'Let's hear what your uncle thinks we should do.'

By now George was on her feet, too. 'I think we

should search right away,' she said. 'He could be listening to us this very minute!'

If you think they should search the island right away, go to **103**.
If not, go to **119**.

115

'I am,' said George in a choky voice. She got up and walked off. 'All right,' she said, over her shoulder. 'I'll leave him on the island with Dad.'

Anne got up to go after George, but Julian pulled her down again.

'Leave her alone! She'll be all right. Good boy, Timmy – you know what you should do, don't you?'

Timmy wagged his tail. He didn't attempt to follow George, because he knew he must stay with her father now.

George came back a few minutes later, just as they were packing up the picnic.

'Dad!' she said. 'If I leave Timmy with you, will you promise to do something for me?'

'What might that be?' asked her father.

'Will you please take Timmy up into the tower with you when you signal in the morning?' George said. 'If I can just catch a glimpse of him, I'll know that he's all right.'

'Very well, George,' said her father. 'I'll take him up with me each morning when I signal, and get him to wag his tail at you!'

Go to **118**.

116

'Well, there was nothing in the big cave,' said George, dropping down on the ground beside her mother. 'Are the other two still looking?'

'Yes,' said Aunt Fanny. 'Would you like a drink

while we wait for them?'

'Yes please,' said George. As her mother handed her a glass of lemonade, she saw Dick and Anne coming towards them.

'Did you find anything?' Julian shouted.

'Yes,' said Dick, as he came up to them. 'Look!'

He held out his hand. On his palm was a piece of newspaper - and at the top of it was the date - the day before yesterday!

'Well,' said Uncle Quentin. 'There's no doubt about it - there *must* be somebody else on this island!'

Go to **119**.

117

Dick and Anne set off for the castle.

'What if we suddenly bump into someone strange?' asked Anne in a worried voice, as they began their search.

'I don't think we will,' said Dick with a laugh. 'After all, if there *is* anyone else hiding on the island, they must know we're here, and they'll take very good care that we don't find them. No – what we're looking for are clues.'

'I wonder if we'd get on better if we had a torch?' said Anne suddenly. 'Some of the corners of the castle are very dark, particularly in the little room.'

'I don't suppose anyone brought a torch with them,' said Dick.

'No – but Uncle Quentin must have one,' argued Anne. 'How could he find his way about after dark otherwise?'

'Anne, you're brilliant!' said Dick, giving her a thump on the back. 'Come on, let's go and ask him!'

They dashed back across the courtyard and down to the little cove.

Go to **109**.

'Uncle Quentin, if anything goes wrong, or you want help, flash eighteen times again,' said Julian. 'You should be safe with Timmy - but you never know.'

'Right,' said Uncle Quentin. 'Now - I think it's time you all left. I must get on with my work.'

Timmy went with them all to the boat, but he didn't attempt to get in. George knelt down beside him and made a fuss of him before she got into the boat. Then she picked up the oars and began to row furiously.

They were only a few yards out from the shore when George suddenly stopped rowing.

'What's the matter, dear?' asked Aunt Fanny.

'I *can't* leave Timmy behind,' said poor George, and she began to pull the boat round so that she could row back to the island.

'George! Stop a minute and listen to me!' said Julian urgently.

George looked at Julian. 'It's no good, Julian,'

she said. 'I must go back!'

If you think Julian can persuade George not to go back, go to **124**.

If you think George ignores him, go to **130**.

119

If you've arrived from **116**, *score* 🐟🐟🐟.

If you've arrived from **113**, *score* 🐟🐟🐟🐟.

There was a silence. Anne felt as if someone was dripping ice-cold water down the back of her neck. George stared at her father, puzzled. Who could be on the island? And why? And how had they got there?

'Well, Quentin – what are you going to do?' asked his wife. 'What would be best?'

'I'll be all right if George will give her consent to something,' said Uncle Quentin. 'I want Timmy here, George. Will you leave him behind with me?'

There was a horrified silence. George stared at her father in complete dismay. Everyone waited to see what she would say.

Go to **111**.

120

'We can look at the map this evening,' said Dick. 'I'd rather go to the farm. Mrs Sanders makes wonderful farmhouse teas,' he added.

'Yes, she does,' agreed Julian. 'I wonder if she's been baking any of those scrumptious scones of hers. Come on, let's go and find out.'

'I'll just tell Mum that's what we're going to do. Won't be a moment,' said George, and she vanished into the kitchen. The others went upstairs to find their raincoats and wellies.

'Mum says that's fine,' said George when she rejoined the others. 'We're to be back by six.'

They walked out of the garden gate and along

the path that led over the moors behind the cottage. They had once found an interesting secret passage at the Sanders' farm, and the farmer and his wife were always glad to see them. When they got there, Julian knocked on the back door.

Go to **123**.

121

'What?' asked everyone.

'Well, do you remember the other day when we first went to see Dad?' asked George. 'He didn't let us stay long, and he came to see us off at the boat. We tried to see where he went – but we couldn't. Dick said he saw the jackdaws rising up in a flock, as if they had been disturbed – and he wondered if Dad had gone somewhere in that direction.'

Julian whistled. 'Yes – the jackdaws build in the tower, which is by the little room – and anyone going into the room would disturb them. I think you're right, George.'

'I wonder how Dad found the hiding-place,' said George thoughtfully.

'Do you suppose the unknown enemy on the island knows Uncle Quentin's hiding-place?' asked Anne, suddenly. 'Oh, I do hope he doesn't!'

'Well, it's no good worrying about it,' said Dick. 'Uncle Quentin's got Timmy with him, so he'll be all right. I think we've solved the mystery, too! However, we won't know for certain until your father's finished his experiment, George, and left the island - then we can go over and have a good look round.'

'Well, it's stopped raining,' said Anne, looking out of the window. 'It looks as though the sun will be out soon. Let's go for a walk.'

'Let's go up to the coastguard's cottage,' said George. 'Then I can look at the island through his telescope, and perhaps I'll see Timmy!'

'We'll all come with you,' said Dick. 'And I don't mind telling you what we'll see!'

‘What?’ asked George in surprise.

‘We’ll see Timmy having a perfectly wonderful time, chasing every single rabbit on the island’ said Dick with a grin. ‘Come on, all of you!’

Go to **129**.

122

‘I’ve come for Timmy, Dad,’ said George. ‘I know you want him to guard you, but I simply can’t leave him behind. If only you’d let me stay with you, everything would be all right.’

Uncle Quentin glared furiously at his difficult daughter, but before he could say anything, Julian and Dick came running into the courtyard.

‘George!’ said Julian. ‘Don’t be so ridioulous! You told your father that you would leave Timmy here – you must keep your word.’

George shook her head. ‘I’m sorry, Julian,

but I can't do it,' she said firmly. 'Timmy! Come here, Timmy!'

Then a very strange thing happened. Timmy refused to budge! He sat down by George's father and would not move, no matter how many times George called him.

At last George gave up.

'It looks as though Timmy has decided to stay here!' she said, with a shaky laugh.

Go to **127**.

123

Julian waited for a short time, and then knocked again, but there was no reply.

'Looks as though they're not in,' said Julian. 'We'd better go back to Kirrin Cottage and decide what else we could do this afternoon.'

Just then one of the farm workers came round the corner of the house.

'Hello,' said Julian. 'Can you tell me if Mr and Mrs Sanders are in?'

'I'm afraid not,' said the man. 'They've gone into town – it's market day. They won't be back for a while yet.'

'Thank you very much,' said Julian, and the four set off home, feeling rather disappointed.

'What shall we do now?' asked George. 'It's such a dreary afternoon, especially without Timmy.'

'We could go and see Mr Curton and Martin. Perhaps they'd let us watch television again,' suggested Anne.

'Or we could go home and play cards,' said Julian.

If you think they should decide to visit the Curtons, go to **128**.

If you think they should go home, go to **134**.

124

Julian leaned forward and took hold of George's arm, forcing her to stop rowing.

'Listen,' he said. 'We all know how much you hate having to leave Timmy behind, but your father really does need him. Don't go back – it'll only make things worse for you and for Timmy.'

George looked at Julian in silence for a moment. Then she pulled the boat round again and started to row furiously towards the mainland.

Go to **133**.

'I remember that we hunted pretty hard for the entrance in the little room,' said Dick. 'We scraped away the weeds from every single stone, and gave up at last. Then we found the other entrance, and forgot all about this one.'

'*I* think Dad has found the entrance we *didn't* find,' said George triumphantly. 'It leads underground, obviously. Whether or not it joins up with the dungeons we know, I can't make out from this map. It's a bit blurred here. But it's clear that there *is* an entrance here, with stone steps leading underground somewhere. See, there's some sort of passage or tunnel marked, leading from the steps. I can't see where it goes, it's so smeared.'

'It joins up with the dungeons, I expect,' said Julian. 'We never explored all of them, you know – they're so vast. If we explored the whole place, we'd probably come across the stone steps leading from somewhere near that little room. Still, they may be ruined or fallen in now.'

'No, they can't be,' said George. 'I'm sure that's the entrance that Dad has found. I'll tell you something that seems to prove it, too!'

Go to **121**.

126

It was only half past one when they arrived back, because they had had lunch quite early. Aunt Fanny gave them some biscuits, and the four children took them into the sitting-room. As they munched, they talked about what they would do that afternoon.

'Let's go and explore the passage in the old quarry,' suggested George.

Julian looked out of the window.

'It's about to pour with rain,' he said. 'I don't think that clambering up and down the steep sides of that quarry in the wet would be very easy. No – we'd better leave that for a fine day.'

'What about going over to Kirrin Farm to see if

Mr and Mrs Sanders are in?' suggested Dick. 'We haven't seen them yet this holiday.'

'I've got an idea!' exclaimed Anne. 'Why don't we have a look at that old map of Kirrin Castle that we found once? Now that we know there's another hiding-place somewhere, we might be able to trace it on the map!'

If you think they should visit the farm, go to **120**.
If you think they should look at the old map, go to **131**.

127

'Now perhaps you will go back to the boat and go home,' said Uncle Quentin. 'You can see Timmy has decided that it's his duty to stay with me. Go home and don't disturb me any more!'

'Come on,' said Julian, grinning at George. 'Timmy's made up his mind, and you're going to have to go along with it!'

George allowed Julian to lead her back to the

boat. She jumped in without saying anything, and started to row furiously away from the island.

Go to **133**.

128

'There's a really good television programme on this afternoon – Martin told me,' said Anne. 'Let's go and see the Curtons.'

'I'd rather go home,' said Dick, making a sullen face.

'Oh, you've just got a thing about Martin and his father,' said Anne. 'Come on – don't be a spoilsport.'

In the end, they decided to walk up to the Curtons' cottage and see if they were in. They were halfway there, when Anne tripped over a stone and fell headlong into a puddle! The others helped her up. Her face and hands were dripping wet, and the front of her anorak was covered in mud.

'Here, dry off with this,' said Julian, offering her his handkerchief. 'Are you all right?'

'Yes, I'm fine, thanks,' said Anne, laughing, 'but I don't think I can go visiting the Curtons, looking like this.'

Go to **134**.

129

By the time they reached the coastguard's cottage, the sun was out. It was a real April day, with sudden showers and then sunshine. It was quite wet underfoot, but the children were wearing wellies.

They looked for the coastguard. He was in his shed, busily hammering.

'Hello, all of you,' he said. 'How nice to see you. How do you like this model railway station I'm making?'

'It's better than anything I've seen in the

shops,' said Anne admiringly. The coastguard certainly had made it well, down to the last detail.

He nodded his head towards some small wooden figures of porters and guards and passengers.

'Those are waiting to be painted,' he said. 'That boy Martin said he'd come in and do them for me. He paints very well indeed. By the way, did you know he's had an accident?'

'*Has* he? What happened?' asked Julian.

Go to **132**.

130

Julian leaned forward and took hold of George's arm, forcing her to stop rowing.

'Listen,' he said. 'We all know how much you hate having to leave. Timmy behind, but don't go back – it'll only make things worse for you and for Timmy.'

Aunt Fanny began to get angry.

‘Please stop behaving like a baby, George,’ she said. ‘You agreed you would leave Timmy with your father, and you know that he needs the dog, so why are you making all this fuss? Just get on and row us home. I’ve got a lot to do.’

George took no notice of Julian or her mother, but continued to row back to the island. As soon as the bottom of the boat bumped on the sand, she jumped out and started to try and pull it up the beach. Then she ran towards the castle, ignoring her mother’s instructions to stay where she was.

When George reached the courtyard of the castle, her father was standing looking at the tower where the jackdaws nested. Timmy was sitting at his feet. The big dog stood up and wagged his tail when he saw George, but he didn’t move.

‘Timmy!’ called George. ‘Timmy! Come here!’

George’s father turned round and saw her.

‘George!’ he shouted. ‘What do you think you’re doing? Go back to Kirrin and take the others with you!’

Go to **122**.

131

If you've arrived from **134**, *score* 🐟🐟🐟.

'That's a really good idea of yours, Anne,' said Julian, and Anne beamed. 'Where *is* the map, George? You have still got it, haven't you?'

'Yes,' said George. 'It's upstairs in my room. I'll go and get it.'

She disappeared upstairs, and came down again with the map. It was made of thick parchment, and was yellow with age. She laid it out on the table. The others bent over it, eager to look at it again.

It was in three parts, a plan of the dungeons, a plan of the ground floor, and a plan of the top part.

'It's no good bothering about the top part of the castle,' said Dick. 'There's practically none of it left, apart from one tower.'

'Look!' said Julian suddenly, putting his finger on a certain spot on the map, 'do you remember there were *two* entrances to the dungeons? One that seemed to start somewhere near that little stone room – and the other that started where we did at last find the entrance? Well – we never found the first entrance, did we?'

'No! We didn't!' George said in excitement. She pushed Julian's finger away from the map. 'Look – there are steps shown here – somewhere where that little room is – so there must be an entrance there! Here's the other flight of steps – the ones we did find, near the well.'

Go to **125**.

132

'I don't quite know,' answered the coastguard. 'His father half carried him home this morning. Must have slipped and fallen somewhere. I went out to ask, but Mr Curton was in a hurry to get the boy to bed.'

'That's a shame,' said Julian. 'We'd like to look through your telescope again, if you wouldn't mind.'

'Not at all,' said the coastguard. 'Help yourselves.'

George went to the telescope and trained it on her island. She moved it around, but could see no sign of Timmy or her father. They must be down in his workroom, wherever it was. She looked at the glass room in the top of the tower. That was empty too, of course. She sighed. It would have been nice to see Timmy.

'Well,' said Julian, after they had all had a look through the telescope, 'shall we go next door and see Martin? It's just about to rain again - another April shower!'

'I think we should go home,' said Dick. 'If Martin's not feeling too good, he'd probably prefer to be left in peace.'

If you think they should go and visit Martin, go to **137**.
If you think they should go home, go to **142**.

133

If you've arrived from **127**, *score* 🐟🐟.

The others all talked hard so that George would think they hadn't noticed how upset she was. They discussed the unknown man on the island. It seemed very mysterious indeed that he had suddenly arrived.

'How did he get there? I'm sure that none of the fishermen would have taken him,' said Dick. 'He must have gone at night, and I doubt if there is anyone except George who would know the way in the dark, or even dare to try and find it. The rocks are so close to the surface – one metre off course and any boat would have a hole in the bottom.'

'No one could reach the island by swimming

from the shore,' said Anne. 'It's too far. I honestly do wonder if there is anyone on the island after all. Perhaps that cigarette end was an old one.'

'It didn't look like it,' said Julian.

He fell into thought, puzzling over the various ways that someone could have used to get on to the island unseen. Suddenly he gave a shout, making all the others jump!

'I know!' he said. 'He could have been winched down on to the island from a helicopter! I did hear a throbbing noise one night, which might easily have been a helicopter engine. I wonder if that's the answer?'

'Well done, Julian!' said Dick.

Go to **126**.

134

If you've arrived from **128**, *score* 🐟.

They decided to go back to Kirrin Cottage. After leaving their anoraks and boots in the porch, they went through to the sitting-room.

Dick took a pack of cards out of a drawer. 'What shall we play?' he asked.

'Do you think this might be a good time to look at the map?' said Anne.

Go to **131**.

135

'Well, if you could go next door and get me the little figures that the coastguard wants me to paint, that would be brilliant,' said Martin. 'Do stay and have tea with me, too. My father won't be back for ages.'

Julian went and got the little figures, and the tins of paint, and put them on a table beside Martin. He was very good at painting the little figures, quick and deft, and Anne sat watching him in admiration. George went to hunt in the larder for the tea things. She cut some bread and butter, found some new honey, brought out a huge chocolate cake and some ginger buns, and put the kettle on to boil.

'This is fantastic,' said Martin as George brought the tea things in. 'By the way, George, where's your dog? Where's Timmy?'

Dick looked at George. He didn't think it would matter telling Martin where Timmy was, so long as George didn't give the *reason*.

George, however, had decided not to mention that Timmy was over on the island.

'Oh, Timmy?' she said airily. 'We left him behind today. He's all right.'

Go to **141**.

136

If you've arrived from **146**, *score* ⊂⊲.

'You'd better do some work,' said Julian. 'At least then you won't have to worry about it any more.'

Dick got his books and settled himself at the table beside his brother. Anne went to help Aunt Fanny sort out some clothes. Just before half past ten Julian went up to his bedroom to watch for the signal from his uncle. A few seconds after the half hour the flashes came - one, two, three, four, five, six - good! Now George would settle down for the day. Perhaps they could go to the quarry in the afternoon. Julian went back to his books.

At about five minutes to eleven there was the sound of running feet and panting breath. George appeared in the door of the dining-room. She was red in the face and breathless.

'Julian! Dick! Something's happened - Timmy's wasn't there!'

Go to **149**.

137

If you've arrived from **142**, *score* 🐟.

'If Martin can't go out he'd probably like some company,' said George. 'Come on!'

They trooped through the gate of the cottage next door to the coastguard's house. As they walked up the path, they heard an angry voice.

'Well, you can't! Always wanting to mess about with a brush and paint. I thought I'd managed to get that idea out of your head. You lie still and get that ankle better! Twisting it just when I want your help!'

Anne stopped, feeling frightened. It was Mr Curton's voice they could hear through the open window. He was obviously giving Martin a good telling off about something. The others stopped too, wondering whether to go in or not.

Then they heard a bang, and saw Mr Curton leaving the cottage from the back door. He walked rapidly down the garden and made for the path that led to the back of the cliff. There was a road there that went to the village.

Go to **144**.

138

'I don't think that would be a very good idea,' said Julian. 'Your father hates being disturbed when he's working, you know he does.'

'What do you think, Dick?' asked George.

'Well, I don't see why you couldn't row over to the island and have a quick look,' said Dick. 'It would put your mind at rest, wouldn't it?'

George got up.

'You're right, Dick,' she said. 'I'm going to go over there. Do either of you want to come with me?'

'I will,' said Dick, who was eager for any excuse to

get away from his books. 'What about you, Julian?'

Julian shook his head. 'I'm going to stay and finish my work,' he said. 'I don't think you should go, George. Uncle Quentin will be furious.'

'I don't care how angry he gets,' said George grimly. 'I must find out what's happened to Timmy!'

Go to **148**.

139

Martin hesitated.

'I'm afraid I did,' he said at last. 'I didn't think it would matter. I'm sorry.'

'Bother!' said Dick. 'That was our own little discovery. We wanted to go and explore it this afternoon, but we thought it would be so wet that we'd fall down the steep slope.'

Julian looked at Martin sharply.

'I suppose that's what happened to *you*?' he said.

'You tried clambering down, and slipped!'

'Yes, I did,' admitted Martin. 'I'm really sorry if you thought it was a secret. I just mentioned it to my father out of interest - you know - something to say, and he wanted to go down and see for himself.'

'I suppose journalists are like that,' said Dick, 'always wanting to be on the spot if there's anything to be ferreted out. It's their job. All right, Martin, forget it, but do try and head your father off the quarry if you can. We *would* like to explore before anyone else finds it!'

There was a pause. Nobody quite knew what to say. Martin was rather difficult to talk to.

'Aren't you bored, lying here?' asked Anne, feeling sorry for him.

'Yes, very,' answered Martin. 'I wanted my father to go and ask the coastguard to bring in some little figures I said I'd paint for him, but he refused. I love painting, you know. I'd rather paint than do anything else in the world!'

This was the longest speech Martin had ever

made to the children. His face lost its dull, bored look as he spoke, and became bright and cheerful.

'Do you want to be an artist?' asked Anne in excitement.

'More than anything,' said Martin, 'but my father doesn't think it's a proper job – he wants me to become a solicitor or something like that.'

'It's very hard on you,' said Julian. 'I wish we could do something to help.'

Go to **135**.

140

Next morning dawned bright and sunny again. George gazed out of the dining-room window at breakfast time wondering if Timmy was running about on her island.

'Dreaming about Timmy?' asked Julian. 'Never mind – you'll soon see him, George. Another hour or so and you can feast your eyes on him through the coastguard's telescope.'

'Do you really think you'll be able to make Timmy out, if he's in the tower with your father?' asked her mother. 'I wouldn't have thought you'd be able to.'

'Yes, I will, Mum,' replied George. 'It's a very powerful telescope, you know. I'll just make my bed, then I'll go up the cliff path. Anyone else coming?'

'I want someone to help me,' said her mother. 'I'm sorting out some old clothes to give to the vicar's wife for her jumble sale.'

'I'll help,' said Anne at once. 'What are the boys going to do?'

'I think we should do some of our holiday work,' said Julian with a sigh.

'I want to go with George,' said Dick.

If you think Dick should do as Julian suggests, go to **136**.
If you think he should go with George, go to **146**.

141

'Gone out shopping with your mother, I suppose?' said Martin. 'He's probably hoping she'll be visiting the butcher.'

The children all laughed as they settled down to a huge tea. Then, when the clock said quarter to six, the girls carried the painted figures back to the coastguard, who was delighted with them. Dick took back the little tins of paint, and the brush.

'Well now, he's very clever, isn't he?' said the coastguard in delight. 'These figures look wonderful!'

'Could I just have one more squint through your telescope, please?' asked George.

'Yes, of course,' said the coastguard.

George tilted the telescope towards the island, but there was no sign of Timmy, nor of her father.

'Can you see anything, George?' asked Dick.

George shook her head. 'No, not a thing,' she said sadly.

Just then there was a knock on the door.

'I expect that's Julian, coming to tell us it's time to go home,' said Anne.

If you think it's Julian, go to **147**.

If you think it's someone else, go to **153**.

142

Julian hesitated.

'You may be right, Dick,' he said at last. 'We'd better go home. Thank you for the use of your telescope, coastguard!'

The coastguard smiled.

'That's all right,' he said. 'Come up any time you like.'

The four children made their way back down the cliff path towards Kirrin Cottage. Aunt Fanny came hurrying to meet them.

'There you all are!' she exclaimed. 'I'm afraid I've got to run down to the village to see the vicar's wife. I'll be gone for some time, and I think you'd better wait for tea until I get back.'

The children looked at each other in dismay.

'How long do you think you'll be, Mum?' asked George.

'At least an hour and a half,' said her mother, bustling ahead of them into the kitchen. She took off her apron and reached for her raincoat. 'I'll be as quick as I can,' she said, and rushed off.

'Well, what shall we do?' said Anne. 'Has anybody got any ideas?'

'Perhaps we could go and see Martin after all,' suggested Julian.

Dick looked a bit doubtful. 'Do you think he'll want to see anyone?' he asked.

Go to **137**.

143

The strange man seemed unwilling to accept that the coastguard had no rooms to let.

'Fine view you must have of the bay and the island,' he said. 'I'd really like to find a room with a view like that.'

'Well, I'm afraid you won't find it here,' said the coastguard, who was beginning to get rather cross. 'I'm sorry I can't help you. Good day to you!'

Very reluctantly, the man turned away, and the coastguard closed the door.

'That was very odd,' said Anne. 'I wonder who could have told him that you let rooms? Everyone in Kirrin must know that you don't.'

Dick said nothing, but he felt rather uneasy. He had a vague feeling that he had seen the man before, but he couldn't remember where. Just then there was another knock on the door.

Go to **147**.

'Good, he's gone. *And* he didn't see us!' said Dick. 'Who would have thought that such a genial, smiling man could sound so unpleasant when he loses his temper?'

They knocked on the door. 'It's us!' called Julian cheerfully. 'Can we come in?'

'Oh, yes!' shouted Martin from indoors, sounding pleased. Julian opened the door and they all went in.

'Hello, Martin!' said Julian. 'We heard you'd had an accident. What happened? Have you hurt yourself badly?'

'No, but I've twisted my ankle and can't walk very easily,' answered Martin. 'Silly thing to do!'

'You'll soon be OK,' said Dick. 'Where were you when you fell?'

Martin suddenly went red, to everyone's surprise.

'Well – I was walking on the edge of the quarry with my father, and I slipped and rolled a good way down,' he said.

There was a silence. Then George spoke.

'I hope you didn't give away our little secret to your father? You didn't tell him about that hole under the shelf of rock, did you?'

Go to **139**.

145

If you've arrived from **148**, *score* 🐟🐟.

'No,' said Julian immediately. 'Don't be so silly, George. Nothing is wrong, except that your father's been forgetful. He's signalled as usual, so we know everything's OK. You mustn't go over there and make a scene.'

'Well, I'll try and be patient,' said George with a sigh, and she got up and went out of the room.

George didn't moan about her worries. She went about with an anxious look in her blue eyes, but she had the sense not to tell her mother how worried she was at not seeing Timmy in the glass room when her father signalled.

She mentioned it, of course, but her mother took the same view as Julian.

'There! I knew he'd forget to take Timmy up with him! He's so forgetful when he's working.'

Go to **152**.

146

'Don't you think you'd better do some work, Dick?' said Julian with a slight frown. 'You'll only get into a panic if you leave it all until the last minute.'

'Oh, I'll get it done some time,' said Dick. 'It's too nice a morning to stay indoors!'

The four of them went upstairs and made their beds, then Julian collected his books while Dick and George got ready to go out. He was settling himself at the dining-room table when he heard them yelling goodbye, and then the front door slammed.

George and Dick enjoyed the walk up the cliff path. They could see the tower on Kirrin Island glittering in the spring sunshine. George had stopped to look at it when she heard Dick gave an exclamation of annoyance.

'Oh darn!' he said.

'What's the matter?' asked George.

'The strap on one of my sandals has broken,' said Dick. 'My ankle turned over on that slippery bit of the path, and the end of the strap has come away from the shoe. I'll have to go back to Kirrin Cottage, George. I can't walk up to the coastguard's cottage like this. Don't wait for me, otherwise you might miss seeing your father and Timmy.'

George went on, while Dick turned back to the cottage.

'What happened to you?' asked Julian, when Dick appeared in the dining-room.

Dick explained about his shoe.

Go to **136**.

147

If you've arrived from **143**, *score* 🐟🐟.

The coastguard opened the door, and Julian came in.

'Come on, all of you,' he said. 'It's time to go home. I can see Mr Curton coming back.'

None of them felt that they liked Mr Curton very much, after hearing how hard he was on Martin, so they were anxious not to run into him.

Saying goodbye to the coastguard, they walked home. Later that evening they played Monopoly, and at bedtime George sat on Julian's bed until half past ten, waiting for her father's signal. Right on time they saw the first flash.

'One,' counted George, 'two – three – four – five – six.' She waited anxiously to see if there were any more, but there weren't.

'Now you can go to bed in peace,' said Julian with a grin. 'Goodnight, George. See you in the morning.'

George went back to her own room, and was soon sound asleep.

Go to **140**.

148

George rushed out of the room like a whirlwind, and Dick ran after her. Julian heard them both going upstairs to change their shoes.

George knocked on the door of her mother's bedroom. Aunt Fanny and Anne were sorting clothes for the church jumble sale.

'I'm just going over to the island, Mum,' said George. 'I won't be long. Dick's coming with me.'

Before Aunt Fanny had a chance to say anything, George was rushing downstairs again.

Aunt Fanny dropped the pile of clothes she was

holding and went over to the window. She opened it and leaned out. George and Dick were running down the front path.

'George!' called her mother. 'Come back here! You are *not* going over to the island. Now don't argue with me!'

George hesitated, wondering whether to disobey her mother and go anyway.

'Do as you are told, Georgina,' said Aunt Fanny, in a tone of voice that George knew was absolutely final.

'Come on, George,' Dick muttered. 'We'd better do as your mother says.'

They went back into the dining-room where Julian was working. George told him what Aunt Fanny had said.

'I know there's something wrong,' she finished. 'Do you think I should sneak out while Mum's busy?'

Go to **145**.

149

The two boys stared at George.

'What do you mean?' asked Julian in surprise. George slumped down in a chair, still panting. They could see that she was trembling, too.

'It's serious, Julian! I tell you, Timmy wasn't in the tower when the signals came!'

'Well – it only means that your absent-minded father forgot to take Timmy with him,' said Julian calmly. 'What *did* you see?'

'I had my eye glued to the telescope,' said George, 'and I saw someone come into the little glass room at the top of the tower. I looked for Timmy, but he wasn't there! The six flashes came – the man disappeared, and that was all! Oh, I do feel really worried, Julian.'

'Well, don't be,' said Julian soothingly. 'Honestly, I'm sure your father just forgot about Timmy. Anyway, if you saw *him*, obviously things are all right.'

'I'm not thinking about Dad!' cried George.

'It's Timmy I'm worried about. Why, even if Dad forgot to take him, he'd go too, you know he would.'

'Your father might have shut the door at the bottom and prevented Timmy from going up,' suggested Dick.

'He might,' said George, frowning. 'I hadn't thought of that. Oh dear – now I shall worry all day. *Why* didn't I stay with Timmy? What shall I do now? Do you think I should go over to the island and see if anything's wrong?'

If you think George should decide to go over to the island, go to **138**.
If you think she should decide to stay at home, go to **145**.

150

Bedtime came. The girls got into bed at about quarter to ten. Anne was tired and fell asleep at once. As soon as George heard her regular breathing she crept quietly out of bed and dressed again. She pulled on her warmest jumper, got her anorak, wellies, and a thick rug, and tiptoed out of the bedroom.

At the top of the stairs she paused. As in most old houses, the stairs in Kirrin Cottage creaked terribly. Aunt Fanny was still up – George could see the light shining from the sitting-room door – and might hear George coming downstairs. Fortunately her mother had the radio on.

'I'll just have to hope for the best,' George said to herself, and began to creep downstairs. The

sitting-room door was ajar, and enough light came from round the door for George to be able to pick her way across the hall towards the door. Giving a sigh of relief, she put her hand on the doorknob, and at that moment she dropped her wellies! Bending down to pick them up, she collided with the hall table, which made a terrible scraping noise on the stone floor!

To George's horror, the sitting-room door started to open wider. She wondered frantically whether she should dash back upstairs, or stand still and try to think of some explanation to give her mother.

If you think she should go back upstairs, go to **158**.

If you think she should stay where she is, go to **163**.

151

If you've arrived from **154**, *score* ⬭.

This time George was able to slip down the stairs

and across the hall without trouble. Out she went into the night. There was a bit of a moon in the sky, so it was not as dark as usual. George was glad – she would be able to see her way through the rocks now – though she was sure she could guide the boat even in the dark!

When she reached the boat she threw her anorak, boots and rug into the stern, then pushed the boat off. Jumping in, she began to row strongly away from the shore. She frowned as she rowed. Had she brought everything she might want? Two torches, plenty of food, a tin opener, something to drink, and a rug to wrap herself in that night.

Go to **155**.

152

The children decided to go to the quarry that afternoon and explore the tunnel under the shelf of rock. They set off after lunch, but when they got to the quarry, they didn't dare to climb down the steep sides. The heavy rain of the day before had made them far too slippery and dangerous.

'Look,' said Julian, pointing to where the bushes and smaller plants were ripped up and crushed. 'I bet that's where Martin fell down the other day! He might have broken his neck!'

'Yes,' said Dick. 'I don't think we should try and go down until it's as dry as it was the other day.'

They were all disappointed. They had brought torches, and a rope, and had looked forward to a little excitement.

'Well, what shall we do?' asked Julian.

'I'm going back home,' said George unexpectedly. 'I'm tired. You others go for a walk.'

'I'll come with you, George,' said Anne, but George shook her head.

'No, thanks, Anne. I'd like to be alone.'

Go to **156**.

153

The coastguard opened the door. A strange man was standing on the step. He was tall and dark, with a beard and glasses, and he was wearing a very shabby raincoat.

'Can I help you?' said the coastguard.

'I heard from someone in the village that you let rooms to summer visitors,' said the man, 'and I wondered if any of them were vacant.'

The coastguard stared at him in surprise.

'Who could have told you that?' he said. 'I don't let rooms – there are only two bedrooms in this cottage. I use one of them, and I keep the other one free for my son when he comes down at weekends.'

Dick was watching the man closely, and could see that he kept trying to see beyond the burly form of the coastguard into the room. There was something about him that Dick didn't like, something sinister.

'The person I spoke to seemed quite certain that you had a room to let,' said the stranger again.

'Well, they might have been talking about the cottage next door,' replied the coastguard, 'but it's not mine, and it's let for three months at the moment anyway.'

Go to **143**.

154

'Well, I think you'd better go back to bed, dear,' said her mother. 'You'll probably catch cold if you go and sit on the cliffs at this time of night. I appreciate that you're worried about Timmy, but catching cold won't help him, will it?'

'No, Mum,' said George. 'Goodnight.'

'Goodnight, dear,' said Aunt Fanny. She went back into the sitting-room and closed the door. George walked back upstairs. She had no intention of going back to bed. She stood at the top of the stairs and counted to one hundred to give her mother time to settle down again with her book.

Luckily the radio was still on, and would cover the noise of the door being opened. George took a deep breath and started down the stairs.

Go to **151**.

155

Back at Kirrin Cottage, Julian lay in bed watching for his uncle's signal. Promptly at half past ten it came. One – two – three – four – five – six flashes! Good!

He wondered why George hadn't come into his room to watch for them. She had last night. He got up, padded to the door of George's room and put his head in.

'George!' he said softly. 'It's OK. Your father's signals have just come again.'

There was no reply. Julian could hear the sound of regular breathing. He was rather surprised. If George was sound asleep, she couldn't be as worried about Timmy as all that, otherwise she would have been lying awake, waiting for the signal.

Julian went back to bed, and was soon asleep. He had no idea that George was at that very moment battling through the waves to Kirrin Island!

Go to **160**.

156

'Well, we'll go over to the cliff, then,' said Julian. 'It'll be nice and windy up there. See you later, George!'

They went off. George turned and sped back to Kirrin Cottage. Her mother was out. George went into the larder and took several things from it. She bundled them into a bag and then fled out of the house.

She went down to the beach where her boat was waiting, and tucked the bag out of sight under one of the seats, then went home.

'I can't help it if what I'm doing is wrong,' she whispered to herself. 'I *know* something isn't right with Timmy, and I'm not at all sure about Dad, either. I'll have to go across to the island. I can't help it if it's wrong!'

The others wondered what was up with George when they came back from their walk. She was so fidgety and restless. They had tea, then did some gardening for Aunt Fanny. George's thoughts were so far away that twice her mother had to stop her pulling up seedlings instead of weeds.

Go to **150**.

157

If you've arrived from **167**, *score* ◯.

The noise came again. It was a curious grating noise, followed by a slight thud. It came from the recess where the fireplace used to be. George sat perfectly still, straining her eyes and ears.

She saw a beam of light in the fireplace recess, and then she heard a man's cough! Was it her father? She listened hard. The beam of light grew brighter. Then she heard another noise – it sounded as if someone had jumped down from somewhere! Then a voice!

'Come on!'

It was not her father! George grew cold with fear. What had happened to her father – and to Timmy? Just then someone else jumped down into the recess, grumbling.

'I'm not used to this crawling about!'

George was almost faint with horror. So there were *two* unknown enemies! The men walked out of the little stone room without seeing George. She guessed they were going to the tower. How long would they be? Should she follow them, or should she search for the place they had appeared from?

If you think she should follow them, go to **164**.

If you think she should search for the entrance, go to **169**.

158

George decided to make a dash for it. She flew across the floor and up the stairs, her heart pounding. Having got far enough up to be invisible from the hall, she waited for the light to be turned on and her mother to appear. But nothing happened!

George waited for what felt like an hour, though her watch told her it was only five minutes. Then she decided to venture far enough to see if the sitting-room door was still open. Peering over the banister, she could see that the door was wider open than it had been. Her mother must have got up and opened it a bit to get some air into the sitting-room! George breathed a huge sigh of relief.

Go to **151**.

159

One of the men coughed, and spoke more loudly.

'No – we won't go down to the cove until later,' he said. 'I'd rather get some sleep, wouldn't you?'

The reply was too quiet for George to hear, but evidently the other man didn't want to go to sleep. George's eyes were used to the dark now, and she saw the men walk over to the tower, unlock the door, and disappear inside.

George stood in the dark courtyard and thought furiously. At first she decided to lock the men in the tower, but when she ran across the courtyard and looked at the door, she found the men had locked it from the inside. Then she wondered whether she ought to row back to Kirrin and get help, but she was worried that something might happen to her father and Timmy while she was gone. She walked back to the little room, trying to think what she should do.

Go to **169**.

160

George was finding it more difficult than she had expected to row over to the island. The moon really didn't give very much light, and it had an annoying habit of going behind a cloud just when she badly needed every scrap of light. But, deftly and cleverly, she managed to make her way through the passage between the hidden rocks. Thank goodness the tide was high, so that most of them were well below the surface.

At last she swung the boat into the little cove. Here the water was perfectly calm. Panting a little, George pulled her boat up as far as she could. Then she stood in the darkness and thought hard.

What was she going to do? Should she take the rug on to the beach and try to get some sleep, waiting until it was light before trying to find her father, or should she go up to the little stone room straight away?

If you think she should sleep on the beach, go to **166**.

If you think she should go up to the little room, go to **171**.

161

George went cautiously down the stone steps. They were steep and narrow. 'I should think they run right down in the middle of the stone wall,' thought George. 'Here's a narrow bit!'

It was so narrow that she had to go sideways. 'Lucky I'm not fat,' she thought. 'Oh – the steps have ended!'

She had got the rug round her shoulders, and had picked up her bag on the way down. In her other hand she held the torch. It was terribly dark and quiet down there. George didn't feel scared because she was hoping to see Timmy at any moment. No one could feel afraid with Timmy just round the corner, waiting to welcome them!

She stood at the bottom of the steps, her torch showing her a narrow tunnel. It curved sharply to the left.

'Now, will it join the dungeons from here?' she wondered, trying to get her sense of direction to help her. 'They can't be far off, though there's no sign of them at the moment.'

She went on down the narrow tunnel.

Go to **165**.

162

George moved round the walls, examining them in the light of her torch. No – there was no sign that a hidden way lay behind any of those stones either. It was most tantalising. If only she knew!

She sat down and wrapped the rug around her for warmth. She was shivering as she huddled there in the dark, trying to puzzle out where the hidden entrance could be.

Then she heard a sound! She jumped, and then stiffened. What was it? Where had it come from? George couldn't decide whether the noise came from inside the little room, or outside in the castle courtyard. She hesitated, wondering whether to stay where she was or go outside and have a look round.

If you think George should stay where she is, go to **157**.
If you think she should go outside and have a look, go to **167**.

163

Before George could move, her mother came out of the sitting-room and turned on the hall light.

'George!' she exclaimed in surprise. 'What are you doing? Why aren't you in bed? Why are you carrying that rug?'

George swallowed hard.

'Well – er – it's like this, Mum,' she said. Suddenly inspiration came. 'I wanted to go up and sit on the cliffs to wait for Dad's signal at ten-thirty. I sort of thought I might feel closer to Timmy like that.'

It sounded like a feeble explanation to George, but Aunt Fanny, knowing how devoted George was to Timmy, didn't think it particularly odd.

'You'd get frozen,' she said.

'Yes, I realise that, Mum,' said George. 'That's why I brought a rug to take with me.'

Go to **154**.

164

George decided to follow them. Luckily she had trainers on, which made no sound as she slipped out of the room after the men. Though she couldn't see them because there was no moonlight, she could hear them. Their shoes clattered on the stones in the courtyard.

George moved into the dark place at the bottom of the jackdaw tower, and stood still. The men seemed to be heading towards the tower in the middle of the courtyard, but suddenly the footsteps stopped. George heard a match being struck, and saw a flare of light as one of the men lit a cigarette. She wasn't close enough to see either of the men's faces, but she heard one of them speaking.

George strained her ears to hear what was said, but the man was speaking very quietly, and she couldn't. She did hear one of the men mention the cove, and her blood ran cold! If they went down to the cove, they would find her boat!

Go to **159**.

165

In one place the roof of the tunnel came down so low that she almost had to crawl. She shone her torch on the walls, and saw that they were made of black rock, which had evidently been too hard to be removed by the tunnel builders long ago.

The tunnel went on and on and on. George was puzzled. Surely by now she must have gone by all the dungeons? Why – she must be heading towards the shore of the island. How strange! Didn't this tunnel join the dungeons then? A little further and she would be under the sea bed itself.

The tunnel took a steep slope downwards. More steps appeared, cut roughly from rock. George climbed down them cautiously. Where in the world was she going?

At the bottom of the steps the tunnel seemed to be cut out of solid rock – or else it was a natural passage, not man-made. George wasn't sure. Her torch showed her black rocky walls and roof, and her feet stumbled over an irregular rocky path.

'I must be very deep down,' she thought, pausing to shine her torch around once more. 'Very deep down, and very far from the castle! Oh no – what's that awful noise?'

Go to **168**.

166

Suddenly overwhelmed with tiredness, George decided she would lie down on the beach and have a sleep before going any further. She spread the rug out on the sand, then lay down on top of it and pulled the sides over herself. In no time at all she was sound asleep.

Though George was very tired, she didn't sleep for long. The sand felt soft when you picked some up and let it run through your fingers, but it made a very hard surface to lie on. After about an hour she awoke, stiff and cold.

'I don't think I'm going to get much sleep if I stay here,' George said to herself. 'I'm so cold, too, and thirsty. Well, at least I can do something about that!'

Reaching in her bag, she pulled out a tin of orangeade and drank it all thirstily. Putting the empty tin back in her bag, she stood up and folded the rug, while trying to decide what to do next.

Go to **171**.

167

George decided to go outside and have a look round. Grasping her torch firmly, she slipped out into the courtyard. Then she stood still and listened intently. The night was absolutely quiet, apart from the faint noise of the waves breaking against the shore of the little island.

Turning on her torch, George began to work her way round the courtyard. She was not sure what she was looking for, but hoped to see some clue to the whereabouts of her father's work room. From time to time the torchlight caught the tower in the middle of the courtyard. The shiny walls gleamed in the light. George walked over to it and tried the door, but it was locked.

In the end George decided to go back to the little room. As far as she could tell in the dark, none of the stones in the courtyard had been disturbed. Everything was just as it always was. She went back into the little room and sat down again, leaning her back against the wall. Tired and cold though she was, she was dropping off to sleep when she was suddenly jerked wide awake!

Go to **157**.

168

George listened. She heard a muffled booming and moaning. Was it her father, doing one of his experiments? The noise went on and on, a deep, never-ending booming.

'I think it's the sea!' said George, amazed. She stood still and listened again. 'Yes – it *is* the sea – over my head! I'm under the rocky bed of Kirrin Bay!'

Poor George suddenly felt scared. She thought of the great waves surging above her, she thought of the restless, moving water scouring the rocky bed over her head, and felt frightened in case the sea should find a way to leak down into the narrow tunnel!

'Don't be silly,' she told herself sternly. 'This tunnel has been here under the sea bed for hundreds of years – why should it suddenly become unsafe now?'

Talking to herself to keep her spirits up, she went on. It was strange to think she was walking under the sea. So this was where her father was at work, under the sea itself.

George suddenly remembered something her father had said to them when they first visited him on the island. What was it now? Oh yes!

'He said he had to have water *above* and *around* him!' she thought. '*Now* I see what he meant! His work room is somewhere down here – so the seawater is *above* him – and it's all *round* the tower, because it's built on an island!'

So that was why her father had chosen Kirrin Island for his experiment. How had he found the secret passage under the sea, though?

'Even I didn't know it was here,' thought George. 'Hmm, which way do I go now?'

The rocky tunnel forked left and right in

front of her.

If you think George should go left, go to **173**.
If you think she should go right, go to **180**.

169

If you've arrived from **159**, *score* 🐟 🐟.

George decided to search for the place the men had appeared from. Her hands were trembling as she turned on her torch. She went to the fireplace and flashed the light in it.

She gave a gasp! Halfway up the chimney at the back was a black opening! She shone the light up there. Evidently there was a movable stone halfway up that swung back and revealed an entrance behind. An entrance to what? Were there steps such as were shown on the old map?

Feeling quite breathless, George stood on tiptoe and shone her torch into the hole. Yes – there were steps! They went down into the wall at the back. She remembered that the little stone room backed on to one of the immensely thick old walls still left.

'I'll have to go down the steps,' she said to herself. 'I'll bet Timmy and Dad are down there somewhere. I'd better take my bag and the rug, in case the men come back and see them. I wonder if this entrance leads to the dungeons?'

She lifted the bag and rug and pushed them into the hole. She heard the bag roll down the steps, the tins inside making a muffled noise.

Then she climbed up herself. What a long dark flight of steps! Wherever did they lead?

Go to **161**.

170

George banged her head as she fell and lay stretched out on the floor of the passage, feeling sick. She remained still with her eyes closed until the dizzy sickness passed off, then she opened her eyes and sat up slowly.

The passage was absolutely pitch black, of course. Not a flicker of light penetrated it. George felt as if she still had her eyes closed. A horrible feeling of panic began to creep over her as she thought of the sea overhead, and the miles of tunnels that she could wander in, getting so lost that she would never find her way back to the entrance.

'Stop it!' she said to herself firmly. 'First of all, I must try and find my torch. It might still work!'

Crawling on her hands and knees, she began to feel around. She moved very slowly, not wanting to bang her head on the walls again. She was also very nervous about moving forwards, since she had no idea where the passage led. There might be a sudden drop!

George was just beginning to despair of ever finding the torch, when suddenly her hand brushed against it! Thankfully, she picked it up and tried to turn it on, but nothing happened.

Go to **175**.

171

If you've arrived from **166**, *score* 🐟.

George decided to go up to the little stone room. She would put on her torch when she got there, and hunt round for any likely entrance to the hiding-place. If she found it, she would go in – and what a surprise she would give her father! If Timmy was there he would go mad with delight.

She took the heavy bag, draped the rug over her arm, and set off. She didn't dare turn on her torch, in case the unknown enemy was lurking near. After all, her father had heard him cough at night!

Eventually she reached the little stone room. It was pitch dark in there, of course - not even the faint light of the moon pierced its blackness. George had to turn on her torch.

Putting her bundle down by the wall at the back, she sat down to have a rest, switching off her torch. After a while she got up, and turned it on again. She began to search for the hiding place. Where *could* the entrance be? She shone her torch on to every flagstone on the floor of the room, but not one of them looked as if it had been disturbed. There was nothing to show where there might be an entrance.

Go to **162**.

172

A light! Then perhaps she was coming to the cave where her father must be! She shone her torch round the cave she was now standing in and saw

tins of food, bottles of beer, and a pile of clothes of some sort. Ah, this was where her father kept his stores. She went on to the next cave, wondering why Timmy had not heard her and come to greet her.

She looked cautiously into the cave the light was coming from. Sitting at a table, his head in his heads, was her father! There was no sign of Timmy.

'Dad!' said George.

The man at the table jumped violently and turned round. He stared at George as if he really couldn't believe his eyes. Then he turned back again, and buried his face in his hands.

'Dad!' exclaimed George again, quite frightened because he didn't say anything to her.

He looked round again, and this time he got up. He stared at George in dismay once more, then sat down heavily.

'What's the matter, Dad?' asked George. 'Oh, Dad, what's the matter? Where's Timmy?'

Go to **177**.

173

George decided to turn left. Holding her torch in front of her, she walked along the passage, hoping at every turn to see some sign of her father and Timmy. The floor of the passage was very bumpy, and from time to time she slipped, hampered by the bag and blanket she was still carrying.

The muffled booming of the sea seemed to be getting louder, and at the same time the floor of the passage began to slope up hill. George wondered if she was going to come out in a cave on the edge of the island. The only cave that she knew about was the one they had lived in for a while the year before, but she thought perhaps there might be a tiny cave somewhere else that she had never discovered.

By now George was feeling very tired, and she found it more and more difficult to walk on the rocky bed of the passage. Suddenly she caught her foot on a protruding rock, and fell flat on her face! The torch flew out of her hand, landing with a crash on the passage floor, and the light went out!

Go to **170**.

174

'I'm listening,' said George.

'Those two men were winched down on to the island from a helicopter, to try and find out my secret,' said her father. 'I'll tell you what my experiments are for, George – they are to find a way of using the power of the waves to make electricity. The world will run out of coal and oil one day, but there will always be wave power.'

'What a brilliant idea!' said George.

'Yes,' said her father. 'I want to *give* the secret to the world, but there are men who want my secret for themselves, so that they can make a fortune out of it.'

'That's awful!' exclaimed George. 'Go on, Dad. How did they hear of it?'

'Well, I was at work on this idea with my colleagues,' answered her father, 'and one of them betrayed me to some criminals. When I found out what had happened I decided to come away in secret and finish my experiments by myself. Then nobody could betray me.'

'So you came here,' said George.

'That's right,' said her father. 'I needed water above me and all round me. Quite by chance I looked at a copy of that old map, and thought that if the passage shown there – the one leading from the little stone room, I mean – if the passage there *really* did lead under the sea, as it seemed to show, that would be the ideal place to finish my experiments. So I got my stuff and came here. Now these men have found me!'

Go to **179**.

175

George gave the torch a shake. Then she fiddled with the switch, but it was no good. Her torch was dead.

'What am I going to do without a torch?' she thought miserably. 'There's no light at all down here. I guess I'll just have to try and feel my way back down the tunnel by running my hand along the walls.'

Her bag was still slung over her shoulders, and she opened it to put the useless torch away. As she stuffed it into the bag, her fingers brushed against something, and she started to laugh.

'I am a fool,' she said to herself. 'I'd completely forgotten I'd put two torches in my bag! Thank goodness for that!'

She pulled out the other torch and turned it on.

'Right!' she said to herself. 'Now to finish exploring this tunnel!'

Go to **178**.

176

Just in time George saw a small gap between one set of wires and the next. Holding her breath, she wriggled through as fast as she could, then dropped down on her hands and knees at the entrance to the little tunnel just as her father rushed into the cave.

'George!' he shouted. 'Come back here at once!'

George took absolutely no notice, but started to wriggle along the passage, holding her torch in front of her. Her father was too big to get through the gap in his equipment that she had used, and besides, he was afraid of damaging it.

'I wonder how long it will be before that hot-headed girl realises that if *I* can't get through my equipment, no other adult could,' he said to himself, and settled down to wait for George to reappear.

Go to **186**.

177

'George! Is it *really* you, George? I thought I must be dreaming when I looked up and saw you!' said her father. 'How did you get here? I don't believe it! It's *impossible* that you should be here!'

'Dad, are you all right? What's happened – and where's Timmy?' asked George urgently. She looked all round, but could see no sign of him. Her heart went cold. Surely nothing awful had happened to Timmy?

'Did you see two men?' asked her father. 'Where were they?'

'Oh, Dad – we keep asking each other questions and not answering them!' said George. 'Tell me first – where is Timmy?'

'I don't know,' answered her father. 'Did those two men go to the tower?'

'Yes,' said George. 'Dad, *what's happened*?'

'Well, if they've gone to the tower, we've got about an hour in peace,' said her father. 'Now listen to me very carefully, George. This is important.'

Go to **174**.

178

Walking very carefully, George went on. The passage was still running up hill, but more gently now. The sound of the sea was very loud, and George guessed that the passage was only just under the sea bed.

She came to a point where the floor of the passage flattened out for about a metre, then sloped down slightly. Shining the torch ahead of her, George could see that it came to a dead end!

'Well, that's that,' she said to herself. 'Dad and Timmy certainly aren't down here. I'll just have to turn round and go back again.'

Clutching the rug, and still moving very carefully, George made her way back to the place where the passages had divided.

Go to **180**.

179

'Poor Dad!' exclaimed George. 'Can't I help? I could go back to Kirrin and bring the police over, couldn't I?'

'Yes, you could!' said her father. 'You mustn't let those men see you, though.'

'I'll do anything you want me to, Dad,' said George, 'but please tell me what's happened to Timmy!'

'Well, he kept by me all the time,' replied her father. 'Really, he's a wonderful dog, George. Unfortunately, just as I was coming out of the little room this morning, to go up the tower with Timmy and signal to you, the two men pounced on me and forced me back in here.'

'Yes, but what happened to Timmy?' asked George impatiently. Would her father *never* tell her what she wanted to know?

'He flew at the men, of course,' said her father, 'but somehow one of them lassoed him with a rope and caught him. From what I heard them saying afterwards, I think they've taken him to some cave and shut him in there. Anyway, I saw one of them getting some dog biscuits out of a bag this evening, so it looks as though he's alive and kicking – and hungry!'

George took a few steps towards the entrance to the cave.

'I'm going to find Timmy, Dad,' she said. 'I *must* find him.'

'Wait,' said her father. 'Don't go dashing off just yet. I'm sure Timmy's in no danger.'

If you think George should go and look for Timmy, go to **184**.

If you think she should wait, go to **190**

180

If you've arrived from **178**, *score* .

George took the right-hand tunnel. It was very short, and widened out suddenly into an enormous dark cave, whose roof was unexpectedly high, lost in dark shadows. George looked around. She saw strange things that she didn't understand at all – wires, glass boxes, little machines that seemed to be at work without a sound, their centres alive with strange gleaming light.

Sudden sparks shot up now and again, and when that happened a funny smell crept round the cave.

'How weird all this is,' thought George. 'How does Dad understand all these machines? I wonder where he is? I hope those men haven't made him a prisoner somewhere.'

From this strange Aladdin's cave led another tunnel. George went into it. It was much like the last one, but the roof was higher.

She came to another cave, smaller this time, and crammed with wires of all kinds. There was a curious humming sound here, like thousands of bees in a hive. George half expected to see some flying around!

'It must be these wires making the noise,' she said. There was nobody in the cave, but it led into another one, and George hoped that soon she would find Timmy and her father.

She went into the next cave, which was perfectly empty and very cold, then down a passage into yet another cave, which was very small. The first thing she saw beyond this tiny cave was a light!

Go to **172**.

181

Just then her father came running into the cave.

'George!' he shouted. 'What do you mean by dashing off like that? I hadn't finished what I was saying! I hope you haven't touched any of the equipment in here, either. You could do a lot of damage, and might give yourself a nasty shock, too!'

'I've *got* to find Timmy, Dad,' said George desperately. 'I couldn't wait any longer to start looking for him.'

'I know how much you want to find him,' replied her father. 'What I've got to say will only take a moment. Now, just listen, will you?'

Go to **190**.

George decided to make a dash for it. Swinging round, she ran along the passage away from the men, Timmy racing at her heels.

'Hey, come back here!' yelled a voice. 'Come back, or I'll shoot!'

'Don't be a fool!' said another voice, trying to sound pleasant. 'He won't shoot at you – we just want to speak to you!'

George knew perfectly well that the men wanted to do more than just speak to her, but she didn't think the one with the gun would risk shooting at her. He couldn't see properly in the torchlight. She raced on down the tunnel, slipping and sliding but never quite falling.

She had absolutely no idea where she was going – she just hoped she would find a place to hide until the men had got fed up looking for her. Then she could hide Timmy, and try and find a way out.

Suddenly there was a terrible commotion behind her. One of the men had obviously tripped and fallen. George tried to run even faster. A moment later the passage curved round to the left, and she was out of the men's sight.

Go to **185**.

183

George smiled at her father.

'Well, Dad, I'll go and see if I can find Timmy now. I've got to see that he's all right before I go and hide in one of the caves.'

'Very well,' said her father. 'The man who took the dog biscuits went in that direction – still further under the sea, George. But George, how is it you're here, in the middle of the night?'

It seemed to strike her father for the first time that George might also have a story to tell, but George felt that she couldn't really waste any more time – she *must* find Timmy.

'I'll tell you later, Dad,' she answered. 'Now –

where's that book of notes?'

Her father rose and went to the back of the cave. He took a box and stood on it. He ran his hand along a dark ridge of rock, and felt about until he had found what he wanted.

He brought down a slim book, whose pages were of very thin paper. He opened the book, and George saw many beautifully-drawn diagrams, and pages of notes in her father's small, neat handwriting.

'Here you are,' said her father, handing her the book. 'Do the best you can. If anything happens to me, this book will enable my colleagues to give my idea to the world. If I come through this all right, I shall be glad to have the book, because it'll mean I won't have to do all my experiments again.'

George took the precious book and stuffed it into her anorak pocket.

'I'll keep it safe, Dad,' she promised. 'Now I must go and find Timmy, or those two men will be back before I can hide in one of the other caves.'

Go to **188**.

184

George decided she couldn't wait any longer before finding Timmy. Ignoring her father's shouted order to stop, she ran back through the caves till she came to the first one, which had all the odd glass boxes and machines in it. She stopped and looked around. Straight in front of her was the short passage from which she had entered the cave. George knew that it was no good looking for Timmy down there!

She hoped to find another exit from the cave, and so she began to shine her torch round the walls. She was very careful not to touch any of the wires or machines, in case she got an electric shock. Suddenly she saw what she was looking for! There was a small opening, just big enough for a man to crawl into, at the base of the cave wall!

George looked for a way to get past all the bits of her father's equipment that were round the walls, but she couldn't see a gap anywhere. Frantically she ran up and down, looking for a place to squeeze through, before her father could come into the cave and stop her. She could hear him running through the other caves.

If you think George manages to get into the little tunnel, go to **176**.
If you think her father catches up with her, go to **181**.

185

George stood still, gasping for breath. She shone her torch round the passage, and spotted what looked like a ledge up one side of it. It was only a little way off the ground, and looked quite deep. Grabbing Timmy's collar, she told him to jump, and managed to heave him on to the ledge. George scrambled swiftly after him, and pulled him to the back of the ledge. It was much deeper than she had expected, almost like a tiny cave, and pitch black. George pulled Timmy down beside her, and lay in the dark with her heart pounding so hard that she thought the men must hear it!

The next moment she saw a light getting stronger and stronger, then the men ran past her hiding-place.

'He must have gone straight on!' shouted one of them as they raced past.

George forced herself to count slowly to fifty, then she and Timmy jumped off the ledge and headed back down the tunnel.

Go to **189**.

186

George crawled through the tunnel on her hands and knees. It was very slow going, because she had to hold her torch in one hand, which made crawling extremely difficult. She kept having to stop and shine the torch on the walls of the tunnel, to look for passages going off to the side, but she didn't find any. Every few metres she stopped and called Timmy's name, hoping to hear an answering bark, but she heard nothing.

Eventually she stopped and sat back on her heels.

'This is ridiculous. I don't think Timmy can be down here,' she said to herself. Then a thought struck her. 'Oh – I am silly! If Dad couldn't get through the gap in his equipment to follow me, then neither of those men could have done, either! They would never have risked ruining Dad's experiment by barging through the wires and things, so they couldn't have brought Timmy into this tunnel! I'd better go back and find Dad.'

The tunnel was too small for her to turn around, so she crawled out backwards, emerging into the cave where her father was waiting.

'You little fool!' her father shouted. 'Why didn't you want to hear the rest of what I had to say? You could have given yourself a nasty shock if you had brushed against any of my equipment. Now just stand still and listen to me for a moment!'

Go to **190**.

187

Timmy growled suddenly, and the hairs on the back of his neck rose up. George stiffened, and stood listening.

A stern voice came down the passage. 'I don't know who you are or where you've come from – but if you let the dog loose he'll be shot. To show you that I mean what I say, here's something to let you know I've got a revolver.'

Then there came a deafening crash, as the man pulled the trigger, and a bullet hit the roof somewhere in the passage. Timmy and George almost jumped out of their skins. Timmy would have leapt up the passage at once, but George had her hand on his collar. She was very frightened, and tried hard to decide what she should do. Would it be best to stand still, or should she make a run for it?

If you think she should stand still, go to **195**.
If you think she should make a run for it, go to **182**.

188

George went through the cave where she had found her father and into the next one. There was nothing there at all. Then she went on down a passage that twisted and turned in the rock.

Suddenly she heard the sound she had been longing to hear! A whine! Yes, really a whine!

'Timmy!' shouted George eagerly. 'Oh, Timmy, I'm coming!'

Timmy's whine stopped suddenly. Then he barked joyously. George almost fell as she tried to run down the narrow tunnel. The torch showed her a big boulder that seemed to be blocking up a small cave in the side of the tunnel. Behind the boulder Timmy barked, and scraped frantically!

George tugged at the stone with all her strength.

'Timmy!' she panted. 'I'll get you out! I'm coming! Oh, Timmy!'

She tugged again, but the stone refused to move. Eventually she sat back on her heels, almost in tears.

'Oh, Timmy!' she whispered. 'I can't get this enormous stone to move! What shall I do?'

She wondered whether it would be best to keep on trying to move the stone, or if she should go and ask her father to help.

If you think she should keep on trying, go to **193**.

If you think she should go to fetch her father, go to **198**.

189

George hoped that if she moved quickly enough, she could get through the caves that her father was using, and along the passage up to the entrance in the little stone room, before the men caught up with her. Sooner or later they would realise that she had given them the slip, and turn back, but with any luck she would be on her way back to Kirrin by then.

She was just passing the cave where Timmy

had been imprisoned when she heard someone shout at her.

'Here, you! Keep still, or it'll be the worse for you. Remember I've got a gun!'

'Timmy! Back in the cave, *quickly*!' hissed George, hoping desperately that the men hadn't seen Timmy when they were chasing her. It was so dark in the tunnels, even using a torch, that it was very difficult to see anything clearly unless it was right in front of you.

Timmy slipped behind George just as the man shouted again.

'Stand still, or else!'

With a deafening roar, he fired his gun again.

Go to **195**.

190

If you've arrived from **181**, *score* 🐟🐟.
If you've arrived from **186**, *score* 🐟🐟🐟.

Reluctantly, George waited to see what else her father had to say.

'Now, listen,' he said. 'I have a book in which I've made all my notes about this great experiment, which the men haven't found. I want you to take it safely to the mainland, George. Don't let it out of your sight! If the men get hold of it they will have all the information they need.'

'Can't they find everything out just by looking at your wires and things?' asked George.

'They can find out a great deal,' said her father, 'but not quite enough. I can't destroy my book of notes, because if anything happens to me, my great idea would be completely lost. So, George, I shall entrust it to you, and you must take it to your mother, who'll know what to do with it.'

'It's a big responsibility,' said George, a little

nervous of handling a book that meant so much. 'I'll do my best, Dad. I'll hide in one of the caves until the men come back, and then I'll slip back up the passage to the hidden entrance, get out, go to my boat and row back to the mainland. Then I'll deliver your book of notes to Mum without fail, and get help sent over to you.'

'Good girl,' said her father, giving her a hug. 'Honestly, George, you are brave. I'm proud of you.'

George thought that was the nicest thing her father had ever said to her!

Go to **183**.

191

'You can do what you like to me,' George's father shouted, 'but I will *never* give my secret to people like you, who just want to use it to make millions for yourselves!'

'Very well,' said the rough voice. 'We'll leave you

here for a while to think about what we've said. Make no mistake, we are going to have your secret!'

George leant against the wall of the cave, trying to make up her mind what to do.

'I don't dare go into the cave and ask Dad to come and help me,' she thought. 'Those men could come back at any time. I'd better go back and find a way of shifting that boulder. I've *got* to move it.'

She walked back along the passage to the boulder, and spoke softly to Timmy. He gave a whine, to show that he could hear her. Then George started to push and pull at the boulder as hard as she could.

After ten minutes she sat down to rest, mopping her hot forehead. It was no good – she could *not* move that horrible boulder.

'I'll have one more try,' she said to herself, as she got to her feet. 'If I can't do it this time, I'll just have to think of something else.'

Go to **193**.

192

Then George heard her father's voice, anxiously calling from somewhere beyond the man.

'George! Is that you? Are you all right?'

'Yes, Dad!' George shouted back, hoping that her father wouldn't ask anything about Timmy. The man beckoned her to come to him, then he pushed her in front of him and they walked to her father's cave.

'I've brought your boy back,' said the man. 'Silly little fool – thinking he could set that dog free! We've got him penned up in a cave with a big boulder in front of the entrance.'

Another man came in from the opposite end of the cave. He was amazed to see George. The first man explained.

'When I got down here, I heard a noise out beyond this cave, the dog barking and someone talking to him – and found this kid there, trying to set the dog free.'

'How on earth did this boy get here?' said the

other man in amazement.

'Maybe *he* can tell us that!' said the first man, and then, for the first time, George's father heard how George had got there, and why.

Go to **196**.

193

If you've arrived from **191**, *score* .

In desperation, George gave the stone another tug, and it moved a little! She tugged again. It was almost too heavy for her to move at all, but despair made her stronger than she had ever been in her life. Quite suddenly the stone swung to one side, and George just got one of her feet out of its way in time, or it would have been crushed.

Timmy squeezed out of the space left. He flung himself on George, who fell on the ground with her arms tight round him. He licked her face and whined, and she buried her nose in his thick fur in joy.

'Timmy!' she whispered. 'Timmy! I came as soon as I could.'

Timmy whined again and again in joy, and tried to paw and lick George as if he couldn't get enough of her. It would have been difficult to say which of the two was the happier.

At last George pushed Timmy away firmly.

'We've got work to do, Timmy!' she said. 'We've got to escape from here and get across to the mainland and bring help. We'll go back to Dad's cave – and then find another cave beyond his to hide in till the two men come back from the tower. Then we'll creep out into the little stone room and row back to the mainland. I've got a very important book in my pocket, Timmy.'

Go to **187**.

'Now, this complicates matters,' said the other man, looking at George. 'If you don't go home, you'll soon be missed. Maybe someone will come over to the island to see if you're here. We don't want anyone here at the moment – not until we know what we want to know!'

He turned to George's father.

'If you'll tell us what we want to know, and give us all your notes, we'll set you free, give you whatever sum of money you ask, and disappear ourselves.'

'And if I still say I won't?' said George's father.

'Then I'm afraid we'll blow up your machines *and* the tower – and possibly you and your son will be buried down here, and no one will ever find you,' said the man, in a voice that was suddenly very hard.

There was a dead silence. George looked at her father.

'You couldn't do a thing like that,' he said at last.

'Oh, yes, we could,' replied the man.

Her father looked over at where George was sitting.

'Don't tell them anything, Dad!' she said fiercely. 'They won't blow the tower up – they're bluffing!'

Her father sat silent, gazing down at his hands. George knew he was worried about what might happen to her if he didn't give in to the men.

'Don't tell them!' she said again.

If you think he should say nothing, go to **199**.
If you think he should pretend to do what the men want, go to **204**.

195

If you've arrived from **189**, *score* 🐟🐟🐟.

The echoes of the shot went on and on. It was terrible. Timmy stopped growling, and George stood perfectly still, afraid to move for fear of the man shooting Timmy.

'Well,' said the voice. 'Did you hear what I said? If that dog is loose, he'll be shot. I'm not having my plans spoilt now. You, whoever you are, will please come up the tunnel and let me see you, but I warn you – if the dog's with you, that's the end of him!'

'Timmy! Timmy, run away and hide somewhere!' whispered George suddenly. Then she remembered something that filled her with despair. She had her father's precious book of notes with her – in her pocket! Suppose the men found it on her? It would break her father's heart to know that his wonderful secret had been stolen from him after all.

George looked round for a hiding-place, and spotted a narrow ledge of rock. Should she put the notebook on the shelf, and come back for it later, or should she give Timmy the notebook to take away?

If you think she should put it on the rocky shelf, go to **205**.

If you think she should give it to Timmy, go to **200**.

196

George told them how she had watched for Timmy in the glass room of the tower and hadn't seen him – and that had worried her and made her suspicious. So she had come across to the island in her boat at night, and had seen where the men came from. She had gone down the tunnel, and kept on until she came to the cave, where she had found her father.

The three men listened in silence.

'Well, you're a tiresome nuisance,' said the first man to George, 'but you're certainly a son to be proud of. It's not many boys who would be brave enough to run so much risk for anyone.'

'Yes, I'm really proud of you, George,' said her father. He looked at her anxiously. She knew what he was thinking – what about his precious book? Had she been sensible enough to hide it? She did not dare to let him know anything while the men were there.

Go to **194**.

197

George sat slumped at the table, feeling utterly wretched. How terrible that her father was going to have to give his wonderful secret to these men, who would use it to make money for themselves, instead of for the benefit of others. She looked at her father. To her amazement, he was suddenly looking much more cheerful. As she stared at him, he winked at her!

'Dad's got a plan!' George said to herself. 'He's thought of some way of outwitting these horrible men. I wonder what he's up to?'

At that moment the other man came back with a pad of paper and a pen.

'Right, there you are! Now get on with it,' said the first man.

Uncle Quentin picked up the pen and started to write. The men watched for a while, then the first one spoke. 'This is obviously going to take him a long time,' he said. 'We might as well go and get some sleep. After all, neither of them can get away!'

He turned to Uncle Quentin.

'We'll be back tomorrow morning – just make sure you've finished!'

They went out of the cave and left George and her father together.

Go to **201**.

198

George gave the boulder one more useless tug, then decided to go and get her father. She made her way back along the rocky passage, not daring to walk too fast in case she tripped.

As she walked into the empty cave next to the one where she had found her father, she heard the sound of loud, angry voices. George stood as if frozen to the spot.

'I've told you over and over again, I will not give you my secret, no matter how much money you offer me,' said her father's voice.

Thankful for her rubber-soled trainers, George crept silently over to the wall of the cave. Then she worked her way round to a point where she could see a bit of the next cave. She could make out her father, standing by the little table, but not the person he was speaking to.

'Well, we aren't going to leave here without it,' said a rough, angry voice. 'If you won't agree to sell us the secret of your experiments, we'll have to try other ways to persuade you!'

George felt sick. What would the men do to her father? He would never, never agree to sell his wonderful secret, she was sure of that.

Go to **191**.

199

At last Uncle Quentin looked at the men.

'I will never give you my secret,' he said. 'Never!'

The first man shrugged.

'I suggest you reconsider,' he said. 'We'll give you till half past ten tomorrow morning - about seven hours. Then either you tell us everything, or we'll blow the island sky high!'

They went out of the cave and left George and her father together.

As soon as the men were out of earshot, George's father spoke in a low voice.

'What have you done with my book of notes, George?'

Go to **208**.

200

If you've arrived from **205**, *score* 🐟.

Thinking furiously, George decided that the best thing to do would be to give the notebook to Timmy. She hurriedly pushed it into Timmy's mouth.

'Go and hide, Timmy! Quickly, now! I'll be all right!' she whispered.

To her great relief, Timmy, with the book in his mouth, turned and disappeared down the tunnel. How she hoped he would soon find a safe hiding-place!

'Will you come up the passage or not?' shouted the voice angrily. 'You'll be sorry if I have to come and fetch you!'

'I'm coming!' called George, and she went towards the voice. In a moment she was in the beam of a powerful torch. There was a surprised exclamation.

'Good heavens! A boy! Where did you come from, and what are you doing here?'

George's short curly hair made the man think that she was a boy, and she didn't tell him he was wrong. The man held a revolver, but he let it drop when he saw her.

'I only came to rescue my dog, and find my father,' said George meekly.

'Well, you can't move that heavy stone!' said the man. 'A kid like you wouldn't have the strength. You can't rescue your father, either! We've got him prisoner, as you no doubt saw!'

'Yes,' said George, delighted to think that the man was sure she had not been strong enough to move the big stone. She wasn't going to say a word about Timmy. If the man thought he was still shut up in that cave, well and good!

Go to **192**.

201

As soon as she was sure the men wouldn't be able to hear her, George spoke to her father.

'Dad! I know you've thought of a way of outwitting those men! What is it?'

Her father smiled.

'I don't think either of those men are scientists,' he replied. 'That means they won't be able to understand my notes – they'll have to find someone who can explain them. Well, I'm writing out the notes, but leaving crucial bits of information out! They won't be able to use them!'

'Dad!' said George. 'That's brilliant!' Suddenly a thought struck her. 'What if one of the men *is* a scientist? He'll read through your notes and know that something's missing.'

'From various things they've said, I'm fairly certain that neither of them knows much about science,' answered her father. 'Well, I'd better get on and finish these fake notes. Oh, by the way, George, what did you do with my *real* notes?'

Go to **208**.

202

If you've arrived from **213**, *score* .

George decided to try the passage on the right. She walked along rather slowly, shining the beam of her torch round the walls from time to time, looking for more caves or passages. Every few metres she stood still and called Timmy's name, but there was no answering bark. She could only just hear the muffled boom of the sea, and she guessed the passage must be a long way down under the sea bed.

George shivered. She was suddenly aware that she was cold, and hungry, and very tired indeed, but she forced herself to go on walking along the tunnel. She must find Timmy!

Gradually the tunnel ceiling began to get lower, and lower. George had to bend her head, then her back, and finally get down on all fours to make any progress. The floor of the tunnel was very hard on her knees!

Go to **207**.

203

George stood up and shone her torch round the cave. It was enormous – far bigger than any of the other caves she had seen so far.

'It's big enough to be a cathedral,' she said out loud, and the sound reverberated round the great cave. Clutching her torch firmly in her hand, she started to walk round the walls of the cave, looking for another tunnel, or the opening to another cave. From time to time she whistled, and called Timmy's name, but, as before, nothing happened. She sat down on the floor of the cave to rest for a while, and was nodding off to sleep when a horrible thought struck her. How was she going to get back up to the hole she had climbed out of? All thought of going to sleep disappeared. She jumped to her feet and ran back across the cave to the hole.

Looking up at it, George could see that even if she could jump up and get her hands on the edge of the hole, she would never be able to pull her body up. The walls of the cave were too smooth to provide any footholds. George sank down on the floor in complete despair. How was she going to get out of the cave?

She could feel panic rising inside her, and took a deep breath.

'Now, be sensible,' she said to herself. 'There must be another way out of the cave, and if there isn't, you'll just have to get back up to that hole!'

She got to her feet and started to search for another way out of the cave.

Go to **210**.

204

At last Uncle Quentin looked at the men.

'All right,' he said, in a sad, defeated voice. 'I'll tell you what you want to know. I don't mind for myself, but I can't risk George's life.'

George jumped to her feet.

'Dad!' she shouted. 'Oh, Dad, don't tell them anything. I'm not frightened – really I'm not. Don't let them have your precious secret just because you're worried about what might happen to me!'

'Your father has more sense than you, George,' said the first man. 'We mean *exactly* what we say – and don't you forget it!'

'Sit down, George,' said her father wearily. He turned to the men. 'I'll have to write out the methods I used for my experiments – I haven't made any notes I can give you. You'd better find me some paper.'

The first man turned to his partner.

'Go and get him some paper and a pen – there's some in the next cave, I think.'

Go to **197**.

205

George took the little notebook and popped it on the rocky ledge. It was very narrow, but she thought the book would be out of sight. If the men caught either Timmy or her, they wouldn't find the book. She could always come back later and collect it.

'Right, Timmy,' she whispered, 'you go and hide. Quickly!'

'What are you doing down there?' shouted the voice from further down the tunnel. 'I told you to come here. If you don't, I'll just have to come and get you.'

To George's horror, at that moment the little book fell off the shelf and landed at her feet!

Hoping the men hadn't seen what had happened, she bent and picked it up as fast as she could. What on earth should she do with it?

Go to **200**.

206

At about half past four Anne awoke, feeling very hot.

'I really must open the window!' she thought. 'I'm boiling.'

She got up and went to the window. She opened it, and stood looking out. The stars were out and the bay shone faintly.

'George,' Anne whispered, 'are you awake?'

She listened for a reply, but none came. Then she listened more intently. She couldn't even hear George's breathing! Surely George was there?

She felt over George's bed. It was flat and empty. She switched on the light and looked at it. George's pyjamas were still on the bed.

'George has gone to the island!' said Anne, feeling frightened. 'All in the dark, by herself!'

She went into the boys' room. Feeling about for Julian's shoulder, she shook him hard. He woke up with a jump. 'What is it? What's up?'

'Julian! George has gone. Her bed's not been slept in,' whispered Anne. Her whisper woke Dick, and soon both boys were sitting up, wide awake.

Go to **209**.

207

George crawled on, hoping that the passage would soon get wider and she would be able to stand up again, but all that happened was that the tunnel began to slope up hill. She crawled steadily up until she suddenly reached a point where she could feel nothing in front of her!

George found that her head and shoulders were

sticking out of a hole about two metres above the floor of another cave. She shone her torch into the cave, but could see so little that she guessed it must be enormous.

'I can't get into the cave head first,' George said to herself, 'I'll have to turn round somehow so that I can wriggle out feet first and drop down on to the floor of the cave like that. Now – is there room here for me to turn round, or am I going to have to reverse down the tunnel until it's wide enough for me to do it there?'

She very quickly found that the tunnel was much too narrow and steep to turn round in, so she had to crawl backwards until she came to a point where it was wide enough. Going backwards up the slope proved fairly tricky, too, but at last she felt her feet go through the hole into the cave, and she wriggled little by little over the edge until she was hanging by her hands. Then she let go, and dropped down to the floor of the cave.

Go to **203**.

208

If you've arrived from **201**, *score* 🐟🐟.

'Dad, I gave it to Timmy,' whispered George thankfully. 'I *did* manage to get that stone away from the entrance to his little prison – though the men think I didn't! I gave the book to Timmy and told him to go and hide till I fetched him.'

'Good work, George!' said her father. 'Well – perhaps if you went and found Timmy and brought him here, he could deal with those two men before they suspect he's free! He's quite capable of getting them both down on the ground at once.'

'Oh, yes!' said George. 'It's our only chance. I'll go and get him now.'

George took her torch and went into the passage that led to the little cave where Timmy had been. She whistled loudly, and then waited, but no

Timmy came. She whistled again, and then went further along the passage. Still no Timmy.

Go to **211**.

209

'I might have guessed she'd do a fool thing like that,' said Julian. 'In the middle of the night, too - and all those dangerous rocks to row round. *Now* what are we going to do about it? I *told* her she wasn't to go over to the island - Timmy would be quite all right! I expect Uncle Quentin forgot to take him up to the tower with him yesterday, that's all. She might have waited until half past ten this morning - then she would probably have seen him.'

'Well - we can't do anything now, I suppose,' asked Anne anxiously.

'Not a thing,' answered Julian. 'I've no doubt she's safely on Kirrin Island by now, making a fuss of Timmy and having a good old row with Uncle Quentin! Really, George is the limit!'

They talked for half an hour and then Julian looked at his watch. 'Five o'clock. We'd better try and get a bit more sleep. Aunt Fanny will be worried in the morning when she hears about George's latest escapade.'

Anne went back to her room, got into bed, and fell asleep.

Go to **217**.

210

George realised that the best place to start looking for another tunnel was near the one she had come out of – a tunnel on the other side of the cave would probably take her *away* from the direction she wanted to go.

Starting under the hole, she began to walk round the cave wall. She had only gone a short way when she suddenly saw the entrance to another tunnel! A huge feeling of relief swept over George, and she hurried into it. It was straight and wide, and she almost ran along it, still calling Timmy's name and whistling. She came to a place where the passage formed a T-junction with another one, and she turned left – turning right would have led her further out under the sea.

A moment or two later, she found herself back where the passage divided into three. Turning round, so that she faced the three tunnels once more, she tried to decide which way to go. She had just come out of the tunnel on the right.

If you think she should choose the tunnel on the left, go to **219**.

If you think she should choose the tunnel in the middle, go to **213**.

211

George called Timmy loudly. 'TIMMY! TIMMY! COME HERE!' But Timmy didn't come. There was no sound of scampering feet, no joyful bark.

'Oh, bother!' thought George. 'I hope he hasn't gone so far away that he can't hear me. I'll go a little further!'

She made her way along the tunnel, past the cave where Timmy had been, and then on down the tunnel again. Still no Timmy.

George rounded a corner and saw that the tunnel split into three. 'Oh dear! Which one should I take?' George said.

If you think she should take the one on the right, go to **202**.
If you think she should take the one on the left, go to **219**.
If you think she should take the one in the middle, go to **213**.

212

Anne decided that she couldn't leave Mr Curton with a broken leg, even though he was their enemy. Slowly and carefully she began to pick her way down the side of the quarry to the place where he was lying.

'Hurry up, can't you?' shouted Mr Curton through gritted teeth.

'I'm doing my best,' called Anne, sounding rather hurt. 'There's no point in me falling over and breaking *my* leg, is there?'

A moment or two later she slid to a stop beside the injured man. He was lying on his side, with his left leg twisted underneath him. His hands were cut and grazed, and so was one side of his face.

'Now, would you like me to put my jumper under your head, to make you more comfortable!' asked Anne. She had done some first aid at school, and knew that she shouldn't try to move Mr Curton, in case it made him worse.

'I'm lying on a rock,' groaned the man. 'Try and

help me to move away from it.'

'Wouldn't it be better if I put something underneath you to cushion you? I don't think you should move,' suggested Anne.

Go to **221**.

213

If you've arrived from **210**, *score* 🐟.

George decided to take the middle passage. It looked wide and high, with a smooth floor. She walked along, shining her torch on the walls from time to time to see if there were any passages leading off the one she was in, but there was nothing. George realised she was absolutely starving, and thought longingly of the food she'd brought over in the boat. All at once she remembered that she'd pushed a small bar of chocolate into the back pocket of her jeans. Thankfully, she pulled it out and ate it.

The tunnel ran on and on, and the sound of the sea grew louder.

'Must be getting nearer the sea bed,' she said to herself. 'Oh, where *has* Timmy gone?'

In the end, George decided to turn back. She had whistled and called until she was hoarse, and but there was no sign of Timmy.

'I hope he's found a way out of these awful caves!' she thought. 'He's such a clever dog, I'm sure he wouldn't have got lost. I'd better go back and try one of the other passages.'

She retraced her steps to the place where the tunnel divided into three. Turning round, so that she faced the tunnel she had just come out of, she tried to decide whether to turn left or right.

If you think she should take the tunnel on the right, go to **202**.

If you think she should take the tunnel on the left, go to **219**.

Timmy was acting oddly. He kept pawing at Julian and whining. He had been very pleased to see everyone, but he seemed to have something on his mind.

'What is it, Timmy?' asked Dick. 'How did you get here? You didn't swim, because you're not wet. If you came in a boat, it must have been with George – and yet you've left her behind!'

'*I* think something's happened to George,' said Anne suddenly. 'I think Timmy keeps pawing you to tell you to go with him and find her. Perhaps she brought him back in the boat, and then was terribly tired and fell asleep on the beach or something. We ought to go and see.'

'Yes, I agree,' said Julian. 'Aunt Fanny, would it be a good idea to have some hot food ready, in case we find George is tired and hungry? We'll go down to the beach and look. It'll soon be daylight.'

'I'll see what I can do,' said Aunt Fanny. She still looked very worried. 'Oh, what a dreadful family

I've got – always in some scrape or other!'

The three children began to dress. Timmy watched them, waiting patiently till they were ready. Then they all went downstairs and out of doors. Julian turned towards the beach, but Timmy stood still. He pawed at Dick and then ran a few steps in the opposite direction.

'Look – he doesn't *want* us to go to the beach! He wants us to go another way!' cried Julian in surprise. 'All right, Timmy – you lead the way and we'll follow!'

Go to **218**.

215

'No,' said George. 'If they came over here I'm sure they'd never find it. We've looked before. It would mean they might get blown up with the island, too. Dad, this is awful.'

'If only we knew where Timmy was!' said her

father, 'or if we could get a message to Julian telling him not to come. What's the time? Oh dear, it's four o'clock in the morning. I suppose Julian and the others are all fast asleep.'

Julian *was* asleep. So was Anne. Dick was in a deep sleep as well, so nobody guessed that George's bed was empty.

Go to **206**.

216

There was a long silence. Dick and Julian thought hard, while Anne stared at the ground, trying not to cry. At last Julian spoke to Martin.

'You did the right thing to tell us. We may be able to prevent something dreadful, but we'll need your help. We need those spades of yours, and I expect you've got a couple of torches, too. We don't want to waste time going to get things, so will you lend us yours, and will you come with us?'

'Yes, I will,' said Martin in a low voice. 'If we go now, Mr Curton won't be able to follow us, because he hasn't got a torch.'

'Right,' said Julian. 'Anne, go back and tell Aunt Fanny what has happened, will you?'

Anne nodded. 'I don't want to come,' she said firmly. 'Be careful, won't you?'

She stood and watched while the three boys climbed into the hole, led by Timmy. Then she turned and began to climb up the steep side of the quarry. Suddenly, she thought she heard something! Crouching down behind a bush, she peered through the leaves, and saw Mr Curton, standing up at the top. Then she heard his voice.

'Martin! Where are you?'

Though he called several times, there was no reply. Mr Curton began to climb down the side of the quarry, but he slipped and rolled down past Anne. Catching sight of her, he looked astonished, then his look turned to one of fear as he rolled faster and faster to the bottom of the deep quarry. Anne heard him give a deep groan as at last he came to a stop.

'Anne!' he called up to her. 'Anne, I think I've broken my leg. Come and help me, will you?'

Anne hesitated.

If you think Anne should help Mr Curton, go to **212**.
If you think she should ignore him, go to **226**.

217

Julian couldn't sleep – he kept thinking of George and wondering exactly where she was. He'd give her a real telling off when she came back!

He was becoming sleepy when he thought he heard a noise on the landing. He strained his ears, but there was silence, so he turned over on his side to make himself more comfortable. Suddenly he was wide awake again! He had definitely heard a noise. He lay there trying to decide whether he should get up and see what it was, or stay in bed.

If you think he should stay in bed, go to **222**.
If you think he should get up, go to **227**.

218

Timmy ran round the house and made for the moor behind. It was most extraordinary. Wherever was he going?

'This is very strange,' said Julian. 'I'm sure George can't be anywhere in this direction.'

Timmy went on swiftly, occasionally turning

his head to make sure that everyone was following him. He led the way to the quarry!

'The quarry! Did George come here, then?' exclaimed Dick. 'Why?'

The dog disappeared down into the middle of the quarry, slipping and sliding down the steep sides as he went. The others followed as best they could. Luckily it wasn't as slippery as before, and they reached the bottom without accident.

Timmy went straight to the shelf of rock and disappeared underneath it.

'He's gone into the tunnel under there,' said Dick. 'You remember – the one we thought we might explore, and didn't. There must be a passage or something there.'

Go to **225**.

219

If you've arrived from **213**, *score* 🐟.

If you've arrived from **210**, *score* 🐟🐟🐟🐟.

George took the passage on the left. She had not gone very far along it when she found that it also split into three! She stopped.

'I'll get lost in this maze of passages under the sea if I go on,' she thought. 'I don't dare. It's too frightening. TIMMY! TIMMY!'

Her voice went echoing along the passage and sounded very strange indeed. She retraced her steps and went right back to her father's cave, feeling miserable.

'Dad, there's no sign of Timmy at all. He must have gone along one of the passages and got lost! Oh dear, this is awful. There are lots of tunnels beyond this cave. It seems as if the whole rocky bed of the sea is mined with tunnels!'

'Quite likely,' replied her father. 'Well – that's a

good plan gone wrong. We must try and think of another.'

'I wonder what Julian and the others will think when they wake up and find me gone,' said George suddenly. 'They might even come and try to find me here.'

'That wouldn't be much good,' said her father. 'These men will simply come down here and wait, and nobody will know where we are. The others don't know of the entrance in the little stone room, do they?'

Go to **215**.

220

'The coastguard might not be in,' argued Dick.

'You know he usually gets up very early and goes walking along the cliffs. I think we'd better go back to Kirrin Cottage for the stuff.'

'All right,' said Julian. 'Are you coming with us, Anne, or you would like to wait here?'

'I'll come too,' said Anne, who had no wish to be left on her own at the quarry!

With Timmy bounding at their heels, they walked back along the path to Kirrin Cottage.

'I think the first place to look would be in the potting shed,' said Julian. 'We should find a spade in there. Anne, you go into the house and tell Aunt Fanny why we've come back, then come back here.'

'OK,' said Anne, and disappeared towards the back door.

Julian and Dick searched all round the potting shed, but there was no sign of a spade, or any rope!

'How strange,' said Dick. 'Surely Uncle Quentin must have a spade somewhere. He couldn't dig the garden without one.'

'Perhaps he keeps it in the garage,' suggested Julian.

Go to **228**.

221

'Why don't you just do as I tell you, you stupid girl!' shouted Mr Curton. 'I want to move away from this rock I'm lying on. Now, give me your hand!'

Anne shrugged. 'Well, all right,' she said, 'but I really don't think it's a good idea.'

'I wouldn't think, if I were you,' snarled Mr Curton. 'You're not very good at it.'

Anne took hold of Mr Curton's hand and tried to help him as he wriggled about, groaning all the time. Sweat ran down his face, and he was obviously in pain.

'Put your hand under my shoulder!' shouted Mr Curton. 'Now push!'

He was trying desperately to move off the stone, but the slightest effort hurt his leg, and he got more and more angry with poor Anne, who was doing her best to help him. Finally, when he had called her stupid for the third time, she burst into tears.

'You horrible man!' she sobbed. 'I'm not going to

try and help you any more. You can lie there until someone else finds you!'

She started to climb back up the side of the quarry.

Go to **223**.

222

If you've arrived from **227**, *score* 🐟.

Julian put out his hand to switch on the light, but before he could do so, something heavy jumped right on top of him!

He yelled, and Dick woke up with a jump. He turned on the light, and Julian saw what was on his bed! It was Timmy!

'Timmy! How did you get here? Where's George?' asked Julian in astonishment.

'Timmy!' echoed Dick. 'Has George brought you back? Is she here too?'

Anne heard the noise and came in to see what had happened.

'*Timmy!* Oh, Julian, is George back too?'

'No, apparently not,' said Julian, puzzled. 'Look at this. Timmy, what have you got in your mouth? Drop it, Tim, drop it!'

Timmy dropped it. Julian picked it up from the bed.

'It's a book of notes - all in Uncle Quentin's handwriting! What *does* this mean? How did Timmy get hold of it - and why did he bring it here? How extraordinary!'

Nobody could imagine why Timmy had suddenly appeared with the book of notes - and no George.

'It's very strange,' said Julian. 'There's something I don't understand here. Let's go and wake Aunt Fanny.'

So they went and woke her up, telling her everything they knew. She was very worried to hear that George was gone. She picked up the book of notes and knew at once that it was important.

'I must put this in the safe,' she said. 'I know it's

valuable. How *did* Timmy get hold of it?'

Go to **214**.

223

Mr Curton shouted after Anne.

'Come back and help me! I'm sorry I shouted at you!'

Anne took absolutely no notice, but went on climbing steadily up the side of the quarry. When she reached the top she looked down. Cupping her hands round her mouth she shouted loudly.

'You're a really horrible man, and I won't fetch help for you! I don't like you!'

Having got all that off her chest, she shot off at top speed over the moor, towards Kirrin Cottage.

'I must tell Aunt Fanny what the boys are up to. She'll know what to do!'

Go to **233**.

'*Ah!*' exclaimed Dick. 'Now we're coming to it. I *thought* Mr Curton was suspiciously interested in Kirrin Island. What's this present job, then?'

'My guardian will be absolutely furious with me for telling you all this,' said Martin, 'but they're planning to blow up Kirrin Island – and I know your uncle is there, and perhaps George too!'

'How do you know all this?' demanded Julian.

'Mr Curton's been keeping in touch with the chaps on the island through his wireless receiver and transmitter,' explained Martin. 'They plan to get your uncle's secret if they can, but if they can't, they'll blow up the island to prevent anyone else getting it!'

'Well, how will they get away, then?' demanded Julian.

'We feel sure that this hole that Timmy found the other day leads under the sea bed to Kirrin Island,' explained Martin. 'Mr Curton's got an old map which clearly shows that there was a passage under the sea. So the chaps on the island can escape down it, after making all the preparations to blow up the island!'

'I see,' said Julian slowly. 'I see it all very clearly now – and I see something else, too! Timmy has found his way from the island, using that passage you've just told us about – and that's why he's led us back here – to take us to the island and rescue Uncle Quentin and George!'

Go to **216**.

225

Julian bent down and looked under the shelf of rock.

'Timmy obviously wants us to follow him,' he said. 'I'll go first.'

He wriggled into the hole, and was soon in the wider bit, and then came out to the part where he could almost stand. He walked a little way in the dark, hearing Timmy bark impatiently now and then. In a moment or two Julian had to stop.

'It's no good trying to follow you in the dark, Timmy!' he called. 'We'll have to go back and get torches.'

Dick was just wriggling through the first part of the hole. Julian called to him to go back.

'It's too dark,' he said. 'We must go and get torches, and perhaps a rope as well.'

'Right,' said Dick. 'We'll have to go back to Kirrin Cottage and get what we need.'

'It's quite a long way,' said Julian, frowning. 'The coastguard's cottage is nearer, and we should be able to borrow what we need from him – if he doesn't mind us calling on him at this hour.'

If you think they should go back to Kirrin Cottage, go to **220**.

If you think they should go to the coastguard's cottage, go to **231**.

226

Anne decided to ignore Mr Curton's shouts for help. If he had broken his leg, it would mean that he couldn't go after the others, and she would be able to get away quickly. As fast as possible she climbed to the top of the quarry.

'Anne, have you seen Martin?' shouted Mr Curton. 'Look for him and tell him that I need him, will you?' He gave another groan.

When Anne reached the top of the quarry she looked down. She cupped her hands round her mouth and shouted loudly.

'You're a really horrible man, and I won't fetch help for you! I don't like you!'

Having got all that off her chest, she shot off at top speed over the moor.

'I must tell Aunt Fanny. She'll know what to do!'

Go to **233**.

227

Julian heard another creak on the landing, followed by a crash! He jumped out of bed and opened the door. Anne was standing on the landing, wearing her dressing-gown.

'What are you doing?' asked Julian. 'What was that crash?'

'I went back to sleep for a while, but I woke up with a jump – I'm worried about George,' explained Anne. 'I got out of bed to get a drink of water from the bathroom, and I dropped the glass!'

'I'll help you clear up,' said Julian. Together they carefully picked up the bits of broken glass, and Julian put them in the waste-paper basket in his bedroom. Anne got a cloth from the bathroom and mopped up the spilt water.

'Go on, back to bed,' said Julian. 'I'll see you at breakfast!'

Julian went back to his room. He was wide awake now, and lay thinking about George running away to the island. Suddenly the bedroom door began to open!

Go to **222**.

228

'That's a good idea,' said Dick, and they went over to the garage. The garage was incredibly messy, just like Uncle Quentin's study. It was easy to see that it was he who looked after it, and not Aunt Fanny.

The two boys turned the garage upside down, but there was no spade, and only a few odds and ends of rope that would be no use at all.

'That's strange,' said Dick at last. 'I would have thought they'd have some rope – George might need it for the boat.'

Just then Anne stuck her head round the garage door.

'Aunt Fanny says it's no use looking for spades or

rope or anything, because Uncle Quentin took all that kind of thing to the island with him!'

Julian gave a groan. 'We should have guessed he would have done,' he said. 'Never mind, we'll just have to go and see the coastguard instead.'

Go to **232**.

229

'It's all very strange,' said Julian, eyeing Martin. 'But let me tell you this, Martin! *We're* going exploring, not you! If there's anything odd up there, *we'll* find it, not you! We won't allow you or your father to get through the hole, so go and find your father and tell him that!'

Martin didn't move. He went very white, and stared at Julian miserably. Anne went up to him and put her hand on his arm.

'Martin, what is it? Why do you look like that? What's the mystery?'

Suddenly Martin turned his back on them all, and his shoulders began to shake.

'Whatever's the matter, Martin?' said Julian. 'Tell us what's upsetting you.'

'Everything, everything!' said Martin in a muffled voice. Then he swung round to face them. 'You don't know what it is to have no mother and no father – nobody who cares about you – and then . . .'

'But you *have* got a father!' said Dick at once.

'No, I haven't!' shouted Martin. 'Mr Curton isn't my father. He's only my guardian, but he makes me call him my father when we're on a job together.'

'A job? What sort of job?' asked Julian.

'Oh, any kind – all horrible,' said Martin. 'Blackmail, or receiving stolen goods – or helping the men who are after your uncle's secret!'

Go to **224**.

Julian, who was in the lead, stopped suddenly. The beam of his torch had shown up a pile of fallen rocks. Timmy had managed to squeeze himself through a hole in them to the other side, but the boys couldn't.

'This is where the spades come in, Martin!' said Dick cheerfully. 'Take a hand!'

By pushing and shovelling, the boys at last managed to move the pile of fallen rocks enough to make a way past. 'Thank goodness for the spades!' said Julian.

They went on, and were soon very glad of the spades again, to move another heap of rocks. Timmy barked impatiently when they kept him waiting. He was very anxious to get back to George.

Soon they came to a place where the tunnel forked into two. Timmy hesitated. He didn't seem quite sure which one to take.

'It looks as if Timmy can't quite remember

which way to go!' laughed Dick. 'We'll have to choose for him.'

If you think they should take the left-hand fork, go to **235**.
If you think they should take the right-hand fork, go to **243**.

231

'That's a good idea,' said Dick. 'I'm sure he'll help us. Come on then. Anne, are you going to come with us, or would you like to stay here!'

'I'll come with you,' said Anne at once. She didn't like the idea of being left at the quarry on her own.

They scrambled back up the side of the quarry and set off along the path to the coast. They hadn't gone very far when Dick gave an exclamation.

'Look!' he said. 'There's Martin, coming towards us. I wonder what he's doing out so early. Hello, Martin!'

Martin was carrying a couple of spades, and had a coil of rope looped over one of his shoulders.

'Are you going gardening, or something?' asked Anne. 'Why the spades?'

Martin went bright red, and said nothing.

Go to **234**.

232

Calling goodbye to Aunt Fanny, they set off to the coastguard's cottage.

Suddenly Dick gave an exclamation. 'Look, there's Martin! I wonder what he's doing out so early? Hello, Martin! Are you going gardening, or something?'

Martin was carrying a couple of spades, and had a coil of rope looped over his shoulder. He stood still when he saw the children, and his face went bright red. He didn't seem to know what to say.

Go to **234**.

233

If you've arrived from **223**, *score* 🐟 🐟.

Meanwhile, the three boys and Timmy were having a strange journey underground. Timmy led the way without faltering, stopping every now and again for the others to catch up with him.

The tunnel at first had a very low roof, and the boys had to walk along in a stooping position, which was very tiring indeed. After a bit, however, the roof became higher. Julian shone his torch round the walls and floor, and saw that instead of

being made of soil, they were now made of rock. He tried to work out where they were.

'We've come practically straight towards the cliff,' he said to Dick. 'That's allowing for a few turns and twists. The tunnel has sloped down so steeply the last few hundred metres that I think we must be very far underground indeed.'

It was not until the boys heard the odd booming noise that George had heard in the caves that they realised they must be under the sea bed. They were walking under the sea to Kirrin Island! How strange and totally extraordinary it was!

Go to **230**.

234

If you're arrived from **232**, *score* 🐟 🐟.

Julian suddenly walked up to Martin and caught hold of his shoulder.

'Look, Martin! There's something funny going on! What are you going to do with those spades? Have you seen George? Do you know where she is, or anything about her? Come on, tell me!'

Martin shook his shoulder away from Julian's grip, looking extremely surprised.

'George? No! What's happened to him?'

'George isn't a him – she's a her,' said Anne. 'She's disappeared. We thought she'd gone to the island to find her dog, and Timmy suddenly appeared at Kirrin Cottage, and brought us here!'

'So it looks as if George might be somewhere near here,' said Julian. 'I want to know if you've seen her or know anything of her whereabouts.'

'No, Julian, I swear I don't!' said Martin.

'Well, tell me what you're doing here so early in the morning, with spades,' said Julian roughly. 'Who are you waiting for? Your father?'

'Yes,' said Martin very sulkily.

'What are you going to do?' asked Dick. 'Are you going to explore that hole under the rock?'

'Yes,' said Martin again, looking sullen and worried. 'No harm in that, is there?'

Go to **229**.

235

The boys hesitated, then Julian made up his mind.

'Let's try the left fork,' he said.

The tunnel they entered was high and wide, with a smooth floor. It made walking a bit easier, particularly for Martin, with his weak ankle. The boys walked along for a while, then Julian realised that he could only just hear the thunder of the sea above them.

'This passage must be taking us deeper and deeper under the sea bed,' he thought.

Just when they had all begun to wonder if the passage was ever going to lead anywhere, they came out into an enormous cave!

The three boys shone their torches round the walls.

'It's *enormous!*' exclaimed Dick. 'As big as – as a cathedral!'

'The walls are very smooth, too,' said Julian, who had walked over to one side, and was running his hand down the wall. 'The sea must have pounded through here once upon a time!'

Martin said nothing. He was so tired that he sat down on the floor of the cave while Julian and Dick explored.

Go to **238**.

236

Uncle Quentin and the four children crouched at the back of the cave. Timmy growled, but George made him stop at once. She didn't know if the men knew he was free or not.

Quiet footsteps passed across the cave in the

darkness. George listened, straining her ears. She thought she could hear two pairs of footsteps, so that meant that both men were passing through the cave. She thought furiously. Was it worth taking a gamble, and setting Timmy on the men? It was very dark in the cave, and they wouldn't see him approach them. On the other hand, the man with the revolver might take a shot at him - and that would be terrible. What should she do?

If you think George should tell Timmy to attack the men, go to **241**.
If you think she should keep him with her, go to **247**.

237

They all made their way through the cave up to the passage that led to the flight of steps from the little stone room.

The entrance was blocked by a large stone slab. Uncle Quentin felt around it for the lever that would make it swing to one side.

'That's odd,' he said after a while. 'I don't seem to be able to find the lever.'

'Let me try, Uncle,' said Julian. 'Here, Dick – hold this torch for me.' He began to search for the lever. Surely it must be here somewhere!

If you think Julian finds the lever, go to **246**.

If you think he doesn't, go to **252**.

238

Julian and Dick walked round the enormous cave, wondering if they would find another tunnel. Suddenly Dick gave a shout.

'Hey, Julian! Look up there!'

He shone his torch up the wall of the cave. About two metres above the ground there was a hole, big enough for a person to climb through!

'Do you think that would lead to another tunnel, or is it just a little recess?' asked Dick.

‘Can’t really say,’ said Julian. ‘It’d be very difficult to climb up to it, because the walls are so smooth. I think we should go and look for another exit.’

‘I think we should explore this one, before we go any further,’ argued Dick.

If you think they should explore the hole in the wall, go to **245**.

If you think they should look for another tunnel, go to **250**.

239

The next moment the beam of a very powerful torch was sweeping round the cave. They were all picked out in its light.

‘Call off that dog!’ said the man with the torch. ‘I’ve found my gun, and I warn you, I won’t hesitate to use it if you don’t do as I say. Call off that dog!’

George dared not disobey. She couldn’t see Timmy – she was completely dazzled by the strong light from the torch – but she called him.

'Timmy! Timmy, come here!'

'Timmy came bounding over to her and rubbed his head against the back of her hand.

'Now, don't try a stunt like that again,' said the man.

He turned off the torch, and the listening children could hear scuffling sounds, which probably meant the man with the gun was helping his friend to his feet.

They heard footsteps again as the two men walked towards the exit from the cave.

Go to **247**.

240

'If you crawl back, Dick,' called Julian, 'I'll try and catch your legs.'

'No, don't do that,' came Dick's voice, sounding

rather muffled. 'I should be able to drop to the floor of the cave without any trouble.'

Julian moved away, and the next minute Dick's legs appeared above his head. They looked so funny that Julian found himself roaring with laughter.

'What's the joke?' asked Martin, limping over to where Julian was standing.

Julian gestured upwards with his torch, and Martin began to laugh too. The legs gave a convulsive heave, and Dick landed in a breathless heap on the floor of the cave.

'What are you two laughing at?' he said, rubbing his elbows, which had got scraped on the tunnel floor.

'Your legs looked so odd, waving about in the air,' said Julian.

'Well, you'd better stop laughing and decide what we're going to do next,' said Dick.

Go to **254**.

241

George made up her mind.

'Get them, Timmy!' she whispered.

The big dog didn't need to be told twice. He flew across the cave at the men, his sharp sense of smell telling him exactly where they were.

There was a muffled crash as the revolver flew out of the man's hand on to the floor of the cave, and a loud curse. Timmy was growling ferociously. None of them dared turn on a torch. They had to sit in the dark and listen to the frantic struggle going on only a few metres away.

The two men had fallen over one another when Timmy flew at them, and the big dog had one of the men pinned on the ground. However, the second man had managed to get to his feet, and was groping round the floor of the cave, looking for the gun that he had dropped when he fell. At last his hand brushed against something made of metal. It was the revolver. He picked it up and scrambled to his feet.

Go to **239**.

242

'I've been given seven hours to say whether or not I will give up my secret,' said Uncle Quentin. 'That time will be up just after half past ten. Then the men will come down and see me again, and I think we should be able to capture them – especially since we've got Timmy with us!'

'Yes – that's a good idea,' said Julian. 'We could hide somewhere until they arrive, and then set Timmy on them before they suspect anything!'

Almost before he had finished speaking the light in the cave went out! A voice spoke out of the blackness.

'Keep still! One move, and I'll shoot.'

George gasped. What was happening? She held Timmy's collar, afraid that he would fly at the man in the darkness and be shot. The voice spoke again.

'Will you or will you not give us your secret?'

'I will not,' said Uncle Quentin quietly.

'You'll let us blow up all your work, and the island, and all of you?' asked the voice.

'Yes! You can do what you like,' shouted George. 'You'll be blown up, too! You'll never get away from the island in a boat – you'd be on the rocks in no time!'

The man in the darkness laughed. It was a very chilling laugh, and it sent shivers down all their spines.

'We'll get away,' he said.

Go to **236**.

243

If you've arrived from **254**, *score* 🐟🐟🐟🐟.

Before Martin or Julian could speak, Timmy darted off down the right-hand tunnel.

'Obviously Timmy's made up his mind that we should go this way!' said Julian. 'Come on!'

The three boys set off again. Dick and Julian were enjoying this strange adventure, even though they were worried about George and Uncle Quentin. Martin, on the other hand, was thoroughly miserable. He said very little, but laboured on after the others. His ankle was still giving him trouble. Dick guessed that he was worried about what would happen to him after the adventure was over. Poor Martin - all he wanted to do was to draw - and instead of that he had been dragged into one horrible job after another by his evil guardian.

Suddenly Julian, who was in the lead, stood still.

'Wait!' he exclaimed. 'Look at this - *three* tunnels. I wonder which one we should take now?'

On the left was a tunnel that seemed to go uphill, in the middle was a tunnel with a stony floor, and to the right was a downhill tunnel.

If you think they should take the one on the left, go to **248**.

If you think they should take the one in the middle, go to **256**.

If you think they should take the one on the right, go to **261**.

244

If you've arrived from **253**, *score* .

If you've arrived from **263**, *score* .

If you've arrived from **258**, *score* .

The three boys retraced their steps to where the four tunnels met. They were growing weary now, and Martin's ankle was hurting him.

'I'm sure we'll find the right way soon,' said Dick comfortingly. 'Now, I wonder which way we should go?'

To their left was the tunnel that led from the quarry, to their right was the tunnel with the stony floor, and opposite them was the tunnel that led uphill.

If you think they should choose the right-hand tunnel, go to **256**.

If you think they should choose the tunnel opposite, go to **248**.

245

Julian hesitated. 'Perhaps you're right, Dick,' he said at last. 'If you stand on my shoulders, you should be able to drag yourself into that hole without too much trouble. Martin and I can bundle Timmy up there, then I'll help him up, and then the two of you can pull me up last.'

'Right,' said Dick briefly.

Julian bent down, and Dick climbed on his shoulders. He had no trouble pulling himself into the hole, though he bruised and scratched his hands in the process. Pulling his torch out of his pocket, he shone it in front of him.

'Hey, Julian,' he shouted. 'It's definitely a tunnel, but it slopes downhill very sharply, and it's so narrow that I can't turn round! I certainly won't be able to help any of you to climb up – there isn't enough room!'

Go to **240**.

246

Julian felt carefully, all around the stone slab. He was just about to give up, when his fingers touched something high above his head.

'Got it!' he cried, clasping the lever with both hands. He pulled hard, but the lever wouldn't budge.

Uncle Quentin looked at it. 'I think they've forced the mechanism somehow, so that the entrance can't be opened from the inside,' he said. 'That's why the lever's been pushed up so much higher than usual.'

'I bet if we all pulled together, we could get it to come down,' declared Dick.

'Or we could find a stone we could hit it with,' said George. 'I'm sure that would move it.'

'I don't think there's anything we can do,' said Julian. 'The stone just can't be moved from this side.'

If you think Dick is right, go to **260**.
If you think George is right, go to **255**.
If you think Julian is right, go to **259**.

247

If you've arrived from **239**, *score* 🐟🐟.

George could feel Timmy straining at his collar, but she didn't dare to let him go. It was just too risky. Those awful men might easily take a shot at him!

As soon as the footsteps had died away, George turned on her torch.

'Dad, those men are going to escape down the tunnel under the sea! We can escape too – but not

that way. My boat is on the shore. Let's go there quickly and get away before they can blow up the island.'

'Yes,' said her father, 'but first I must go up the tower. They intend to use the power there, but if I can get there first, I can undo all their plans!'

'Be quick then, Dad!' exclaimed George, who was getting in rather a panic. 'Save my island, if you can!'

Go to **237**.

248

If you've arrived from **244**, *score* 🐟 🐟.

'Let's try the one that goes uphill,' suggested Martin.

'I think that's as good a place as any to start,' said Julian cheerfully, and the three boys set off along the tunnel, with Timmy running ahead of them.

Gradually the roof of the tunnel became lower and lower. They all had to crouch down to move along. Soon they were on their hands and knees.

'I feel like Timmy,' said Dick. 'Woof! Woof!'

'Where *is* Timmy?' asked Julian. 'Is he behind you, Martin?'

'No, he's not, but listen – I think I can hear him,' said Martin.

They all stayed still. Far behind them they heard Timmy whining. It was an urgent kind of noise, as if he was trying to tell them something.

Go to **251**.

Uncle Quentin and George stared in the very greatest amazement.

'Julian! Dick! And *Martin*! How did you get here?' cried George, while Timmy jumped and capered round her.

'I'll explain,' said Julian. 'It was Timmy that fetched us!'

He told the story of how Timmy had come into Kirrin Cottage in the early morning and jumped on his bed, and all that had happened since. Then, in their turn, Uncle Quentin and George told all that had happened to *them*!

'Where are the two men?' asked Julian.

'Somewhere on the island,' answered George. 'I went scouting after them some time ago, and followed them up to where they got out into the little stone room. I think they're there until half past ten this morning, when they'll go up and signal, so that people will think that everything is all right.'

'Well, what are our plans?' said Julian. 'Will you come back down the passage under the sea with us?'

'Better not do that,' said Martin quickly. 'My guardian may be coming – and he's in touch with the other men. If he wonders where I am, and thinks something is up, he may call in two or three others and we might meet them making their way along the passage.'

They didn't know, of course, that Mr Curton was even then lying at the bottom of the quarry with a broken leg.

Go to **242**.

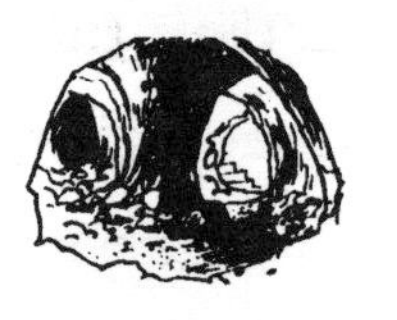

250

'It would be quite difficult to climb up there,' said Julian again.

'Perhaps you're right,' said Dick. 'If we don't find another way out of the cave, we can always come back to this one.' He turned and called to Martin. 'Come on, Martin.'

Martin heaved himself to his feet and joined the others. Then they walked slowly forwards, keeping their torches trained on the wall of the cave. They seemed to have walked almost all the way round the cave when they came to a gap in the cave wall!

'Another tunnel!' cried Julian, with relief. 'Come on, let's try this one!'

The passage was high and wide, with a smooth floor.

'Oh, no!' said Dick. 'This is the tunnel we just came down.'

'We'd better go back down it,' said Julian. 'I don't think there's another way out of this cave.'

Go to **254**.

251

'We'd better go back,' said Dick. 'I think Timmy doesn't like us going this way.'

It was hard work, crawling backwards, but soon they were able to stand up and turn round. They made their way back to where the four tunnels met, and found Timmy waiting for them.

'So we went the wrong way, boy, did we?' Julian gave Timmy a pat. 'Which way now, then?' But this time the dog seemed undecided.

To their right was the tunnel that led to the quarry. Should they now go down the tunnel with the stony floor, or follow the tunnel that went downhill?

If you think they should choose the tunnel with the stony floor, go to **256**.
If you think they should choose the downhill tunnel, go to **261**.

252

‘What sort of lever is it?’ Julian asked Uncle Quentin.

‘A big iron one,’ his uncle replied. ‘About the size of a rounders bat.’

Julian continued to search, with no success, until Dick pointed to a small piece of metal between the stone slab and the wall of the passage.

‘Look,’ he said. ‘I think the lever’s been broken off.’

‘You’re right,’ said Uncle Quentin. ‘Well, we really are trapped now. What shall we do? Any ideas, anybody?’

Go to **259**.

253

If you've arrived from **263**, *score* 🐟🐟.

If you've arrived from **258**, *score* 🐟🐟🐟.

They started to go down the high, narrow passage. After a while, it became even narrower, and Julian had to go sideways.

Suddenly, he stopped, and Dick bumped into him.

'I'm stuck!' he complained. 'Here, pull me out, will you?'

Dick pulled and pulled, and Martin pulled at Dick.

'Ouch!' said Dick. 'You're splitting me in two!'

At last Julian was free. He rubbed his shoulder.

'I don't think we can go any further,' he said. 'I hope this isn't the right way, or we'll never reach George and Uncle Quentin – not unless we lose some weight first!'

'Surely they can't be down there,' said Dick.

'They could be,' explained Julian. 'After all, Timmy

could have come up through quite a narrow space. Oh well, let's go back, anyway.'

They made their way back to the beginning of the passage. They now had three choices: to go down the low, wide tunnel, to try the rounded tunnel, or to go back to where the downhill tunnel had started.

If you think they should go down the low, wide tunnel, go to **266**.
If you think they should go down the rounded tunnel, go to **271**.
If you think they should go back, go to **244**.

254

If you've arrived from **240**, *score* ◯.

They retraced their steps until they arrived back at the fork.

'Which way now?' asked Martin.

'We came along there,' replied Dick, pointing to the tunnel that led from the quarry, 'and chose the left-hand fork. So now we have to try the other one, I suppose.'

Go to **243**.

255

'Let's try George's idea,' said Uncle Quentin.

Martin found a stone on the floor of the passage, and Uncle Quentin, who was the tallest, tried to hit the lever with it. After a while, he gave up.

'It's not moving at all,' he said.

'I still think we should try all together to pull it down,' said Dick. 'I bet that would work.'

'And I still think the stone can't be moved,' said Julian.

If you think Dick is right, go to **260**.
If you think Julian is right, go to **259**.

256

If you've arrived from **251***, or* **244***, score* 🐟🐟.

Before anyone could speak, Timmy trotted confidently into the mouth of the tunnel with the stony floor.

'Timmy seems to know where he's going,' said Julian. 'Let's follow him.'

With Timmy running in front of them, the three boys made their way down the tunnel. It seemed to go on and on, and they were all feeling rather tired by now.

'Do you think we're getting anywhere near the island?' asked Martin wearily.

'Yes, we must be,' said Julian. 'In fact I think we'd better not make any noise, in case we come suddenly on the enemy!'

So, without speaking again, they went as quietly as they could – and then all of a sudden they saw a faint light ahead of them. Julian put out his hand to stop the others.

They were nearing the cave where George's father kept his books and papers - where George had found him. Timmy stood in front of them, listening too. He was not going to run into danger!

They heard voices, and listened intently to see whose they were.

'Uncle Quentin's - and George's,' said Julian at last.

Suddenly Timmy ran ahead of them into the lighted cave, as if satisfied that he recognised the two voices.

'Timmy!' came George's voice. 'Where have you been?'

And then Julian and Dick ran into the cave, followed by Martin.

Go to **249**.

'Where's Quentin gone?' asked Aunt Fanny, sounding very worried. Nobody answered. Julian, Dick, George and Martin were watching the tower with anxious intensity. If only Uncle Quentin would appear at the top. Ah – there he was!

He had taken a very large stone with him, and as they watched, he used it to smash the glass round the tower. The wires that ran through the glass were broken and split as the glass crashed into pieces. No power could race through them now. Uncle Quentin leaned out of the broken glass room and shouted exultantly.

'It's all right! I was in time! I've destroyed the power that might have blown up the island – we're safe!'

George suddenly found that her knees were shaking, and she had to sit down on the ground. Timmy came and licked her face, then sat down beside her.

'What's your father doing, smashing the tower

like that?' asked one of the fishermen. 'I don't understand all this!'

'Neither do I!' said Aunt Fanny.

Go to **262**.

258

Julian inspected the iron band closely. 'It's quite likely these tunnels were once used by smugglers, you know,' he said. 'I think this is a band that went round a cask of rum. Over the years it's become embedded in the floor.'

The others had a close look.

'Do you think this tunnel leads anywhere, Julian?' asked Dick after a while.

'I'm not sure,' replied Julian. 'Perhaps it would be best to turn round and go back.'

The others agreed, so Martin stood up, and they made their way back to the beginning of the passage. They now had three choices: to go down the high, narrow tunnel, to try the low, wide tunnel, or to go back to where the downhill tunnel had started.

If you think they should go down the high, narrow tunnel, go to **253**.
If you think they should go down the low, wide tunnel, go to **266**.
If you think they should go back, go to **244**.

259

If you've arrived from **255**, *score* 🐟.
If you've arrived from **265**, *score* 🐟 🐟.

They sat down on the stone steps in a row, one above the other. They were hungry, cold and miserable. All they could do was to go back down the passage to the mainland, and leave Kirrin Island to its terrible fate.

All of a sudden, Julian stood up.

'Listen!' he said. 'I can hear something outside this wall. Sh!'

They all listened intently. Timmy whined and scratched at the stone that wouldn't move.

'It's voices!' cried Dick. 'Lots of them! Who can it be?'

'Be *quiet*!' said Julian fiercely. 'We *must* find out!'

'I know, I know!' said George suddenly. 'It's the fishermen who have come over in their boats. *That's* why the men didn't wait until half past ten! *That's* why they went in such a hurry! They saw the fishing boats coming!'

'Then Anne must have brought them!' shouted Dick. 'She must have run home to Aunt Fanny, told her everything and given the news to the fishermen – and they've come to rescue us. Anne! ANNE! WE'RE HERE!'

Go to **268**.

260

If you've arrived from **255**, *score* 🐟.

'Let's try Dick's idea,' said Uncle Quentin.

They all stood on the top step, but only Julian and Uncle Quentin could reach the lever. The others tried hanging on to them, but that didn't seem to work very well. Dick slipped and scraped his shin on the step, and George managed to pull Julian's hands off the lever.

Go to **265**.

261

If you've arrived from **251**, *score* 🐟🐟.

'Let's try this one,' said Dick, pointing to the tunnel that led off downhill.

'Well, we've got to start somewhere,' said Julian a trifle wearily, and the three boys started to walk down the dark passage. Martin began to feel almost as if he were having a nightmare about wandering through the tunnels. He very much wished that he was safe in his own bed, even though that would mean that Mr Curton was in the next room!

Suddenly Dick, who was in the lead, gave a groan and stood still.

'What's the matter, Dick?' asked Julian.

'Look!' said Dick, shining his torch ahead of him. The other two boys stared hard in front of them, their hearts sinking. The passage split into three again!

'Now which way shall we go?' asked Martin.

The passage on the left was high and narrow. The one in the middle was low and wide. The one on the right had a rounded shape, like the inside of a large tube.

'Perhaps we should simply go back,' said Julian. 'If we start trying to explore all these tunnels we're likely to get hopelessly lost.'

'Oh, come on Julian,' said Dick. 'It's not like you to give up so easily.'

If you think they should choose the left-hand tunnel, go to **253**.
If you think they should choose the centre tunnel, go to **266**.
If you think they should choose the right-hand tunnel, go to **271**.
If you think they should go back, go to **244**.

262

Uncle Quentin came down the tower and rejoined them.

'Another ten minutes and I would have been too late,' he said. 'Thank goodness you all arrived when you did!'

'I ran all the way home and told Aunt Fanny,' explained Anne. 'We got the fishermen to come over as soon as they could get out their boats. We couldn't think of any other way of rescuing you. Where are those awful men?'

'Trying to escape down the tunnel under the sea,' said Julian. 'Oh – you don't know about that, Anne, do you?' He told her all about it, while the fishermen all listened, open mouthed.

'Look here,' said Uncle Quentin, when Julian had finished, 'as the boats are here, perhaps the fishermen would be willing to take all my gear back with them. I've finished my job here, and won't want to use the island any more.'

'Oh! Then *we* can have it!' cried George in delight. 'There's plenty of the holidays left. We'll help to bring your things up, Dad.'

'We ought to get back as quickly as we can, to catch those chaps at the other end of the tunnel,' suggested one of the fishermen.

'Do you think it would be better to follow them down the tunnel?' suggested George. 'It might be quicker.'

If you think they should go by boat, go to **270**.

If you think they should go down the tunnel, go to **275**.

263

They went forwards a little further, then Julian stopped again.

'It's no good,' he said. 'It's getting wetter and wetter.'

He shone his torch on the floor of the tunnel ahead. It was covered in water, and they couldn't see how deep it might be.

'I think we'd better go back,' said Julian.

They made their way back to the beginning of the passage. They now had three choices: to go down the high, narrow tunnel, to try the rounded tunnel, or to go back to where the downhill tunnel had started.

If you think they should go down the high, narrow tunnel, go to **253**.

If you think they should go down the rounded tunnel, go to **271**.
If you think they should go back, go to **244**.

264

'What's up?' asked Dick. 'Is it your ankle again?'

'No,' answered Martin. 'I tripped over something. Look!'

Julian shone the torch where Martin was pointing. Partly embedded in the floor of the cave was a large iron band.

'What is it?' asked Dick. 'Martin's lucky he didn't cut himself on it.'

'I know what it is,' said Julian.

Go to **258**.

265

‘Perhaps if we could tie something round the lever, we could all pull on that,’ said George. ‘Have you got any rope, Julian?’

‘No, but Martin has,’ said Julian.

Martin produced a length of rope, and Julian tied a noose in one end of it. When they had managed to slip this over the lever, everyone took hold of the rope and pulled.

‘Heave!’ said Uncle Quentin, and suddenly they were all falling backwards down the steps.

‘Have we done it?’ asked Dick. ‘Has the slab moved?’

‘No,’ said Julian, picking himself up. He held something in the air. ‘The lever broke off. It must have been very old and rusty.’

‘Now what are we going to do?’ said Uncle Quentin gloomily.

Go to **259**.

266

They chose the low, wide passage, and had to stoop a little to avoid the jagged rocks in the ceiling.

By the light of his torch, Julian noticed that the walls ahead were shiny. He put out a hand to feel them, and stopped.

'There's water here,' he said.

'Perhaps it's the sea, leaking in,' suggested Dick.

Julian licked his finger.

'No,' he said. 'It's not salty. It's fresh water. Perhaps there's an underground spring. How strange!'

Go to **263**.

267

The police surgeon was with them, and he saw to Mr Curton's leg. Then, with the help of the others, he got the man up to the top of the quarry with great difficulty.

'Julian, why don't you go back to Kirrin Cottage and get some sandwiches,' suggested his uncle. 'It looks as though we're in for a long wait.'

'Good idea!' said Julian, and started to climb the quarry again. In no time he was back with neat packets of ham sandwiches and a flask of hot coffee. The two policemen who were left suggested that Uncle Quentin might like to go home and rest, but he refused.

'Dear me, no!' he said. 'I want to see the faces of these two fellows when they come out. It's going to be one of the nicest moments of my life!'

'I've had a thought, Dad,' broke in George. 'I think the two men are lost underground! Julian said there were a great many passages, but that Timmy helped them to find their way. Well, those two men haven't got Timmy to help them, have they? Perhaps we should send Timmy in to try and find them.'

'Or some of us could go and look for them?'

suggested Dick. 'The policemen could come with us.'

If you think George's idea is best, go to **272**.
If you think Dick's idea is best, go to **276**.

268

Timmy began to bark deafeningly. The others encouraged him, because they felt certain that Timmy's bark was louder than their shouts!

WOOF! WOOF! WOOF!

Anne heard the barking and the shouting as soon as she ran into the little stone room.

'Where are you? Where are you?' she yelled.

'HERE! HERE! MOVE THE STONE!' Julian shouted back.

'Move aside, Anne – I can see which stone it is,' said the deep voice of one of the fishermen.

He felt round and about the stone in the recess, sure it was the right one because it was cleaner than

the others through being used as an entrance. Suddenly he touched the right place, and found a tiny iron spike. He pulled it down – and the stone swung back.

Everyone hurried out, one on top of the other! The six fishermen standing in the room stared in astonishment. Aunt Fanny was there, too. Uncle Quentin brushed past them all and ran towards the tower. Would he be in time to save the island, and everyone on it?'

Go to **257**.

269

Julian went a bit red in the face.

'As a matter of fact, we've solved *lots* of mysteries – haven't we, Dick?' he said. 'We've found some treasure, and caught some smugglers, and rescued a little girl who'd been kidnapped – all sorts of things.'

The policeman looked as if he didn't believe Julian, but Dick said, 'He's absolutely right, Constable. We *have* done all those things.'

'Even so,' said the policeman, 'I see no point in putting ourselves in danger down those tunnels. The men can't escape – we've got people on the island by now, guarding the other end of the tunnel. Sorry, son, but you'll just have to wait.'

Julian told Uncle Quentin what the policeman had said.

'That's all very well,' said Uncle Quentin. 'But we

could be here for hours and hours while they try to find the way out.'

Go to **272**.

270

If you've arrived from **273**, *score* 🐟🐟🐟.

'If we want to head the men off at the quarry, we'll have to go by boat,' said Uncle Quentin. 'Come on, all of you – there's no time to lose! My equipment will just have to wait.'

'I've just remembered something,' exclaimed Anne. 'Mr Curton is lying at the bottom of the quarry with a broken leg!'

The others looked at her curiously, because it was the first they had heard about Mr Curton being in the quarry.

'And I told him he was a very unpleasant man indeed!' Anne finished triumphantly.

'Quite right too!' said her uncle, as they all made their way to the cave.

It was a beautiful day, and the sea was very calm, except just round the island where the waters were always rough. Soon George's boat was moving swiftly towards the mainland.

'Another to add to our list of adventures,' said Julian. 'Cheer up, Martin! Whatever happens, we'll try and see you don't come out badly over this. You helped us, and we don't want you to suffer, do we, Uncle Quentin?'

'Well - thanks,' said Martin. 'If you can get me away from my guardian - and never let me see him again, I'd be very happy!'

'It's quite likely that Mr Curton will be put somewhere he won't be able to see his friends for a very long time,' said Uncle Quentin drily.

Go to **277**.

271

If you've arrived from **253**, *score* 🐟.
If you've arrived from **263**, *score* 🐟 🐟.

The rounded tunnel curved round to the right, then straightened up. Julian shone the torch ahead of him, but the passage seemed to go on for ever.

Suddenly, Martin gave a cry.

The others turned round to see him stumble against the side of the tunnel, then slip down to the floor.

Go to **264**.

272

If you've arrived from ***269****, score* (fish symbol).

'I think we should send Timmy in,' said George again.

'That's an excellent idea,' said Uncle Quentin. 'Go ahead, George!'

'Go in, Timmy!' ordered George, pointing towards the hole under the rock. 'Go and find them, boy, and bring them here!'

'Woof!' said Timmy, and disappeared into the hole.

Everyone waited, munching sandwiches and sipping coffee. Then they heard Timmy's bark again, from underground!

There was a panting noise, then a scraping sound as somebody came wriggling out from under the rock. He stood up – and then he saw the silent group, watching him. He gasped.

'Good morning, Johnson,' said Uncle Quentin in an amiable voice. 'How are you?'

Johnson went white. There was another scraping noise, and then the second man appeared. He stood up – and then he, too, saw the watching group.

'Good morning, Peters,' said Uncle Quentin.

'Careful,' warned Julian. 'Remember they've got a gun!'

Go to **274**.

273

In the confined space of the tunnel, the noise of the shot was shattering. For a minute all the children thought they had gone deaf, and it took them some time to realise that a sinister rumbling noise could be heard!

'Oh help!' exclaimed Dick. 'What's that noise?'

'The bullet must have struck the ceiling of the tunnel,' said Julian. 'I think there's going to be a rock fall. Come on, RUN!'

At that moment there was a tremendous roaring noise, and rocks and earth started to fall into the passage. A choking dust filled the air, making it difficult for the children to breathe.

They flew back the way they had come.

'We'll never catch up with the men now,' panted George. 'We'll have to go back to the mainland by boat and try and catch them in the quarry. Oh no!'

'What's the matter, George?' said Julian, startled by his cousin's shout of dismay.

'What if that rock fall cracked the sea bed?' asked George anxiously. 'If it did, any minute now water will come pouring into the tunnel!'

'I don't think it did,' said Julian calmly. 'The tunnel is very deep under the sea at this point, and I doubt if the shot disturbed more than a metre of rock and earth. Don't worry!'

George felt slightly reassured, but was very thankful when they reached the steps and climbed out into the stone room again. They told her father what had happened.

Go to **270**.

'Not any more,' said Johnson, in a dejected voice. 'Your dog saw to that. Knocked it out of my hand.'

Timmy appeared then, wagging his tail, and went straight up to George.

'All the same, I bet you were glad of Timmy's help,' said Julian.

Johnson looked at him. 'Yes, we were lost in those hateful tunnels. Curton said he'd come to meet us, but he never came.'

'No,' said Uncle Quentin, with a dry laugh. 'He's

probably in hospital by now, with a broken leg.'

The policemen arrested the two men, and the whole company made their way back across the moor. Johnson and Peters were bundled into a police car and driven off, while the rest of the company went into the Kirrin Cottage to have a good meal.

They had a very lively breakfast. Martin, now that he knew he would be free of his guardian, became a different boy. As they ate, they made plans for his future.

'We're going to ask the coastguard if you can stay with him,' said Julian. 'He likes you - he kept on and on saying you weren't a bad boy! Uncle Quentin says he'll help you get into an art school, too!'

Go to **279**.

275

Uncle Quentin hesitated.

'I'm not sure that I want to go down the tunnel

and leave all my equipment – some of it's very important,' he said. 'But perhaps that would be the best way of catching the men. We'll have to hurry, though. They've got quite a start on us.'

'You stay here then, Uncle,' said Julian. 'We'll follow the men.'

'No, you won't,' retorted his uncle. 'Those men have got a gun. I think it's far too dangerous.'

'We've got Timmy, though!' exclaimed George. 'We'll be perfectly all right with him, you know we will.'

'Oh, very well,' said Uncle Quentin, 'but you had better stay here, Anne, and Martin too.'

Anne was only too thankful not to have to start chasing through the dark tunnels. Martin's ankle was hurting him, and he was glad to sit down for a while.

Julian, Dick and George went back through the entrance in the little stone room and down the steps into the tunnel.

Go to **278**.

276

'I'd like to see their faces if we arrive with a couple of policemen,' said Julian. 'Come on, let's ask.'

He and Dick went over to the policemen and told them the plan.

'Well now,' said one of the policemen. 'What have we got here? A couple of would-be detectives, eh?'

Go to **269**.

277

As soon as the boat reached shore, Julian, George, Dick, Timmy and Uncle Quentin hurried off to the quarry to see if Mr Curton was still there – and to wait for the men to come out of the tunnel.

Mr Curton was there all right, groaning and calling for help. Uncle Quentin spoke to him sternly.

'We know your part in this matter, Curton,' he said. 'You will be dealt with by the police, who will be here soon.'

Then they all sat down by the mouth of the tunnel and waited for the men to appear, but nobody came! An hour went by – then another, and still there was nobody.

'I'm glad Martin and Anne didn't come,' said Uncle Quentin, 'but I wish we'd brought some sandwiches!'

At that moment the police arrived, scrambling down the steep side of the quarry.

Go to **267**.

278

The three children rushed along the passage and through the caves where Uncle Quentin had done his experiments. Timmy bounded ahead of them. He seemed to know exactly which way the men had gone, and they raced through the maze of tunnels behind him.

'I hope we're not too late to stop them!' panted Dick.

'They've got quite a start on us,' said Julian, 'but we're a lot younger than they are, and probably, fitter, too!'

At last, just as Julian had begun to wonder if the men had succeeded in getting away, they rounded a slight curve in the tunnel and saw torchlight up ahead.

'Hey, stop!' shouted Julian.

The two men paused and looked behind them.

'You can't get away,' said Julian. 'We've got the dog with us, and he'll see that you don't get any further!'

There was no answer, but a shot rang out in the blackness!

Go to **273**.

Martin glowed with pleasure. It seemed as though a load had fallen away from his shoulders!

After breakfast the Famous Five went out into the garden and looked across Kirrin Bay to Kirrin Island. It was lovely in the morning sun.

'Well, George,' said Julian. 'You've got your island back again.'

'Yes,' said George. 'Let's go there this afternoon.'

'I wonder,' Dick said with a grin, 'what our *next* adventure will be . . . ?'

How many red herrings have you collected?

0–25	Very good indeed! The Famous Five must have been glad to have you with them.
26–50	Promising. Perhaps your next adventure with the Famous Five will be even more successful.
51–75	You took a long time getting there, didn't you? You'll have to do better than that to keep up with the Famous Five!
More than 75	Oh, dear! Perhaps you should go back to the beginning of the story and try again.

Join the Famous Five on more of their exciting adventures.

The Famous Five Adventure
Game Book 1
based on *Five On A Treasure Island*

The Famous Five Adventure
Game Book 2
based on *Five Go Adventuring Again*

The Famous Five Adventure
Game Book 3
based on *Five Run Away Together*

The Famous Five Adventure
Game Book 4
based on *Five Go To Smuggler's Top*

The Famous Five Adventure
Game Book 5
based on *Five Go Off In A Caravan*

Meet Peter, Janet and Jack, Barbara, Pam, Colin and George. Together they are The Secret Seven – ready to solve any mystery, anytime! A great introduction to adventure stories.

For the full range of Secret Seven books and eBooks, please see www.hodderchildrens.co.uk

Elizabeth Allen is spoilt, mischievous and determined to get home – whatever the cost – she really is the Naughtiest Girl in the school! Exciting stories about the girls and boys boarding at Whyteleafe School.

THE FAMOUS FIVE'S SURVIVAL GUIDE

Packed with useful information on surviving outdoors and solving mysteries, here is the one mystery that the Famous Five never managed to solve. See if you can follow the trail to discover the location of the priceless Royal Dragon of Siam.

The perfect book for all fans of mystery, adventure and the Famous Five!

ISBN 9780340970836